MW01681001

Through Smoke and Secrets

Rebecca Hemlock

Copyright © 2026 by Rebecca Coram (Writing as Rebecca Hemlock)

All rights reserved.

No portion of this book may be reproduced in any form without written permission from the publisher or author, except as permitted by U.S. copyright law. *This is a work of fiction. Names, characters, businesses, places, events, locales, and incidents are either the products of the author's imagination or used in a fictitious manner. Any resemblance to actual persons, living or dead, or actual events is purely coincidental.*

Ebook ISBN: 979-8-9908544-8-2

Paperback ISBN: 979-8-9908544-9-9

Hardback ISBN: 979-8-9958514-0-0

Book Cover Designer: Melody Simmons

Bookcoversbymelody.com

Books By Rebecca Hemlock

An Arctic Mystery series

Bitter Betrayal
Deadly Decisions

The Granton house series

The Secret of the 14th Room
The Secret Diary of Deadly Deception
Hidden passages to Dark Secrets

Oakwood Springs PD Series

Fury in the Shadows
Fatal Perception
Lethal Inheritance

Fight to Thrive Series

A Nurse's Revenge
A Nurse's Ambush

Stand-alone

Tailored For Justice

For God gave us a spirit not of fear but of power and love and self-control.

2nd Timothy 1:7 KJV

THROUGH SMOKE AND SECRETS

REBECCA HEMLOCK

Prologue

March 1, 1927
Fairview, Tennessee

The suffering and pain a woman must face is to be borne in silence and with grace. The words echoed in Eleanor Blackwood's mind exactly as Aunt Annabelle used to recite them.

Every day of her childhood, they had crept into her thoughts, branding themselves there until she began to believe them. She had no choice. It was the only way to please the woman who raised her and shaped her into the ideal bride for an eligible bachelor.

Today, fifteen years into her marriage and carrying her third child, she had seen more suffering, by both men and women, than she'd ever thought possible. And yet, for some unspoken reason, society still expected women to endure it quietly. It wasn't right. It couldn't be. How was she supposed to carry such a burden in silence? Worse—alone.

It was nearing six in the morning, a familiar periwinkle hue pushing through the window as the sun crept over the horizon.

She placed one hand on her hip to support her aching back and made her way down the stairs and out to the back garden. A tear slipped down her cheek, and she pressed her lips together to steady their quiver.

The crisp mountain air brushed her skin, a chilly breeze cutting through the stillness. The doctor said fresh air was good for her condition, so she had a ready excuse if Thomas came looking for her.

Her breaths grew heavier, sobs tightening in her throat. No. She had to reach her spot first. Then she could cry. No one must see her.

Suffer in silence. Always suffer in silence.

She placed one hand on her swollen belly and reached the other behind her to steady herself as she lowered onto the stone bench. Only then did she allow the tears and sobs to break free.

The small life inside her fluttered, as if sensing her distress.

"Hush now," she whispered, smoothing her hand over the curve of her abdomen. "Mama will keep you safe. I promise."

But could she?

The question had stolen her sleep for weeks. It had her inspecting her food before every meal, locking her bedroom door at night despite Thomas's reassurances. Why couldn't he understand her fear?

There was no way of knowing whether the child she carried was a boy or a girl. Not yet. But whatever the baby was would determine the danger ahead—not for her, but for this innocent life that had yet to draw its first breath.

At least she knew the source of that danger.

Richard.

Her husband's nephew's words from the previous week still haunted her. He had placed his hand on her belly uninvited, and smiled in a way far too cold for a seventeen-year-old boy.

"Let's hope God blesses you with another daughter, Eleanor," he'd said softly. "For the baby's sake, of course. Sons can cause such... complications."

On the surface, it sounded like concern. Beneath it lay a threat she could not ignore.

When Thomas's father had formed the business, he'd ensured the contracts and deeds were drawn so that only the next male Blackwood could inherit its vast assets upon turning eighteen. Eleanor had already given Thomas two daughters. That meant Richard was the heir—unless this baby was a boy.

Richard had wrapped his warning in silk and false concern, but it was a warning nonetheless.

Thomas hadn't taken it seriously.

That night, in their bedroom, his voice had taken on the patient, condescending tone she'd grown to dread. "Darling, these fears you're having; they're not uncommon in expectant mothers. Nerves. The doctor says it's quite normal for women in your condition to become... overwrought."

Overwrought.

As though she hadn't overheard Richard himself on the telephone, muttering that if she gave birth to a boy, something would need to be done.

"Eleanor," Thomas had continued gently, "Richard would never harm an infant. Especially not his own kin. He's only seventeen, for heaven's sake. Since his mother passed, he's become like my own son."

But Eleanor had seen the calculation in Richard's eyes, the darkness beneath boyish smiles and thoughtful gifts.

Richard would turn eighteen in two weeks.

The baby could arrive before then. And if it was a boy...

She pressed both hands to her belly as the child moved again. "I won't let Richard hurt you," she whispered. "I don't care if your father thinks I'm hysterical. I know what I heard."

A robin landed on the garden wall, its song piercing the quiet morning. Eleanor watched it through blurred vision, her thoughts spiraling. Infants succumbed to natural causes all the time. A pillow pressed too firmly during a fit of crying. Medicine mixed incorrectly. A fall from the arms of a well-meaning cousin.

Accidents happened.

And she would never be able to prove malicious intent.

If there were no male heir, Richard would inherit everything on his eighteenth birthday. She would rather see him named heir now—even if she bore a son—if it meant her child would be safe.

Eleanor wiped her tears with the back of her hand and straightened despite the ache in her spine. If Thomas wouldn't protect this child, then she would. If God chose to give her a son, she would need proof of Richard's guilt should anything happen to Thomas Jr.

Or she could wait for the trap she had already set in motion—one that would reveal Richard's treachery to her husband.

She closed her fingers around the locket resting against her chest and drew in a steadying breath.

Either way, today her silent suffering would end.

Chapter 1

Present Day
Fairview, Tennessee

She'd never come so close to death. It had been only two days since the accident with the black SUV. It was pretty much a hit-and-run. Annie Whitaker had been driving home from the Blackwood estate sale, barely keeping control of her old Honda, when the SUV growled as it pulled alongside her.

Before she could react, it swerved and shoved her car onto the narrow shoulder. The sudden impact nearly sent her over the guardrail. She would have plummeted down the mountainside if she hadn't slammed on the brakes in time.

Her thoughts circled the what-ifs for what felt like the three hundredth time. What if the guardrail hadn't been there? What if she hadn't bought new tires two days earlier? What if she'd been driving just a little faster? The questions made her shiver, her stomach tightening. Uncle Eric had insisted she take a few days to rest, but that wasn't an option.

She forced the thoughts away. This wasn't the time. She was safe now and had work to do.

The glow from her laptop cast eerie shadows across the cluttered studio apartment as Annie rubbed her tired eyes. Boxes and storage bins crowded nearly every surface, each one holding fragments of someone else's life.

The grand opening of her antique shop was less than a week away, and she still had several Victorian pieces to research and price. She'd spent most of the past week consumed by stress—unpacking, cataloging, arranging displays—trying to impose order on chaos. Yet the mess hadn't dampened the familiar thrill that bloomed in her chest each time she uncovered an item she hadn't known she possessed.

She loved that feeling. It was what kept her going.

Exhaustion tugged at her eyelids. She stretched and rolled her desk chair side to side, trying to ease the ache in her back and stiff muscles. How long had she been doing this?

She glanced at the clock in the corner of her screen. Eleven fifteen.

The research on the Victorian jewelry was taking longer than expected. Some pieces were rare, likely to bring a solid profit. Others turned out to be worthless fakes. Frustration had crept in as the evening wore on. She should have spotted them. She knew Victorian jewelry. Rookie mistakes like this weren't an option—not when this shop represented everything she'd worked for over the last three years.

One piece, in particular, held her attention.

A large oval locket set with small green gemstones. On closer inspection, delicate etchings scored the gold surface, aligning the stones with the points of a compass rose.

It felt different from the others—heavier, more significant. She'd noticed it immediately while sorting through a jewelry box from the Blackwood estate sale, tucked beneath tangled costume pearls and brooches. The clasp had stuck when she tried to open it, but she'd managed a brief glimpse of what looked like a small key and a folded slip of paper inside.

Opening it properly without damaging it would take time. That could wait until morning.

She yawned. Definitely time to stop. Today had turned out far crazier than she'd anticipated.

The small wooden cross at the edge of her desk caught her eye. A gift from Uncle Eric when she'd told him about the antique shop.

"Guide me, Lord." she whispered, the same prayer she'd said every night since her parents died.

A soft thud sounded from downstairs.

She froze. There wasn't supposed to be anyone down there.

Her heart slammed against her ribs as she strained to listen. The old building creaked and settled constantly, but this sound was different. Deliberate. Like someone bumping into furniture in the dark.

Lord, help me not let fear control me, she prayed silently, a habit Uncle Eric had taught her after her parents' murder. Give me wisdom to know real danger from imagined threats.

She forced a slow breath.

You're being paranoid.

But paranoia had kept her alive before.

A familiar chill slid up her spine, dragging memories she'd spent years trying to bury. Her parents' faces. Blood on white carpet. The sound of her own screaming.

Another noise drifted up from the shop below—definitely not the building settling.

Footsteps. Slow. Careful. Someone trying not to be heard.

Maybe it was Uncle Eric. He'd been working late, helping her prepare for the opening. He had keys. He knew she stayed up late.

But Eric would have called out to her.

He wouldn't move through the dark like this—especially knowing what she'd endured as a child.

She reached for her phone, then hesitated. What if she was wrong? What if it really was nothing, and she panicked for no reason?

Stop second guessing yourself and follow your gut! Another life lesson from Uncle Eric.

Her instincts screamed danger.

She slipped the locket into the side pocket of her jeans and held her breath, listening.

Silence.

Then the footsteps quickened.

Terror surged through her as she grabbed her phone and crept toward the narrow staircase leading down to the shop. The steps groaned beneath her weight despite her efforts to move quietly, each sound amplified in the darkness.

"Uncle Eric?" she whispered, hope thinning her voice.

No answer.

She edged through the storage room and pressed her back against the wall, peering around the corner into the shop. Moonlight spilled through the front windows, casting long shadows between furniture and display cases. Everything looked normal.

It wasn't.

The air itself seemed to pulse with threat.

A shadow shifted near the back corner, slipping behind the display of Civil War memorabilia.

Her breath caught.

That wasn't Uncle Eric.

The figure was tall, broad-shouldered, and dressed in dark clothing. Something concealed their face—a ski mask or hood. They moved with purpose, rifling through boxes and papers on her desk as if searching for something.

What are they looking for?

She backed toward the stairs, phone slick in her sweaty palm. Her thumb hovered over the emergency button—

The intruder's head snapped toward her.

They made eye contact.

She gasped.

Time fractured as the figure lunged. Annie spun and ran, bare feet sliding on the wooden floor. She caught the handrail and flung herself up the stairs.

The apartment felt impossibly small as she searched for somewhere to hide—or something to defend herself with.

The knife block.

If she could just reach it—

Heavy footsteps thundered behind her. She lunged for the counter, fingers wrapping around the largest knife just as rough hands clamped down on her shoulders.

She twisted—and for a split second, she saw his eyes.

Cold. Focused. Stripped of hesitation.

"Where is it?" The voice was low, distorted by the mask. Male. Unfamiliar.

"Where is what?" She tried to drive the knife between them.

Pain exploded through her arm as he wrenched it back, twisting hard enough to steal her breath. The force turned her away from him, her grip faltering as white-hot agony raced up her shoulder.

He was stronger—and knew exactly where to apply pressure.

The knife flew from her hand, skidding across the floor. He slammed her into the wall, the impact knocking the air from her lungs as his forearm pressed into her throat.

"The locket," he growled close to her ear. "Where is it!!?"

Her thoughts scattered. How could he know about that? She'd only found it today. It had been buried in a jewelry box, forgotten among worthless trinkets.

Unless someone had been watching her.

The black SUV flashed through her mind.

Had the accident been deliberate? Had someone tried to kill her before she ever made it home?

"I don't—"

The pressure on her throat increased. Dark spots danced at the edges of her vision. No, it wouldn't end this way, not without a fight.

She drove her knee up hard. He grunted, loosening his hold just enough for her to wrench free. She stumbled toward her phone, which had skidded across the floor during the struggle.

"Nine-one-one, what's your emergency?"

"Someone's attacking me—" The intruder tackled her from behind, sending them crashing into the coffee table. Pain exploded through her shoulder as she landed on the bits of broken wood and glass.

The phone slid across the linoleum, the dispatcher's voice distant and distorted.

"Ma'am? Are you there?"

She rolled and crawled toward the phone. Her fingers brushed it—

Hands closed around her ankle, yanking her back.

"Ma'am, I'm dispatching units to your location. Stay on the line."

The intruder cursed and released her. He tore through the apartment, desperation evident as boxes crashed and papers scattered.

"It has to be here!" His words came through gritted teeth.

Thank God he hadn't noticed it weighing down her pocket—or heard the faint jingle of its chain when she moved.

She dragged the phone close. "438 Main Street. The antique shop. He's looking for a locket. He—"

The apartment door slammed.

He was gone.

Annie lay on the floor, shaking, listening to the dispatcher's steady voice and the distant wail of approaching sirens.

The locket.

He hadn't been after money. Or electronics. Or the huge pile of expensive jewelry spread across her desk.

He'd wanted the locket.

But why?

And more disturbing still—how did he know she had it at all?

***

Jack Calloway rubbed his burning eyes and leaned back in his desk chair, the cold case file spread across his desk like pieces of a puzzle that refused to fit. The Henley disappearance from 2004 had haunted him for weeks, but tonight the words seemed to blur together on the page.

It had never used to be this hard.

Maybe it was the late hour. Maybe it was working the case alone. Without the fresh perspective that used to make all the difference.

Without Annie.

The thought slipped in uninvited, as it had far too often over the past four years. He'd trained himself not to think about her, not to wonder where she was or whether she was happy. But cases like this, cases that demanded intuition as much as logic made forgetting about her impossible.

They'd been a good team once. More than good.

Annie saw patterns where others saw chaos, connections where others dismissed coincidence. Her mind worked differently than his, and together they'd solved cases that had stumped the department for decades. She always insisted they pray before examining evidence.

"God sees everything, Jack. He already knows the truth we're looking for."

He'd stopped praying after his wife Lily was killed. But with Annie, it felt natural. Right.

The Brennan kidnapping. Cold for fifteen years before they cracked it in less than a month.

The Morrison murders. Three weeks of working together had accomplished what three years of conventional investigation hadn't.

And then he'd ruined it.

He remembered the way she had looked at him during long nights hunched over files and crime scene photos. How she leaned closer when they debated theories, her perfume mingling with the scent of paper and coffee. The way her eyes would suddenly light up when something clicked.

Just thinking about her brought a tight ache to his chest. That pull he'd felt around her wasn't subtle, and the memory twisted through him—sweet, painful, impossible.

He had pushed her away back then. He was too damaged, too afraid to let anyone in again. And even now, he knew she deserved better than a man who woke in cold sweats and saw danger in every shadow. Haunted by the past and things left unresolved.

Ten years ago, when Lily was murdered in Memphis, he'd stopped believing God had a plan for his life. Three years later, when he returned to Fairview broken and faithless, he'd sworn he'd never trust anyone again.

Then Annie came along.

Another three years of working cold cases with her had slowly pulled him back toward both faith and hope. Her quiet prayers. Her certainty that God cared about justice for forgotten victims.

Until the night she told him she loved him and the terror of losing someone else had driven him away from both Annie and God.

The radio crackled, jerking him back to the present.

"Unit Forty-Seven, respond to 438 Main Street. Assault and breaking and entering. Victim secure. Requesting detective on scene."

Jack was already reaching for his jacket before the dispatcher finished. Any excuse to escape the ghosts on his desk was welcome.

The drive took less than five minutes in Fairview, but his mind wandered along familiar streets. He'd lived here most of his life. Every corner, every family, every buried secret.

That was the blessing and curse of small-town policing. Nothing stayed hidden for long and everyone's business became public property.

He parked behind the ambulance and patrol car, noting the small crowd of neighbors gathered despite the late hour. News of violence traveled fast here.

"What do we have?" he asked Officer Martinez at the door.

"Break-in at the antique shop," Martinez said. "Victim's a thirty-three-year-old female. Banged up but nothing serious. Says the intruder was after something specific." He glanced at his notes. "A locket. Suspect fled when she called 911."

"Description?"

"Tall. Broad-shouldered. Masked. Male voice. That's all she could give." Martinez nodded toward the stairs. "She's upstairs. Paramedics cleared her, but she's shaken."

Jack entered through the side door, taking in the narrow staircase at the back of the storage room. As he climbed, his eyes scanned automatically—floor, walls, banister. Anything left behind. Hair. Blood. Fibers.

He paused at the top of the stairs, preparing to introduce himself.

The woman looked up just as he stepped foot into the apartment.

Familiar baby blue eyes stared back at him, sending warmth throughout his body.

Annie.

Her expression shifted in quick succession—recognition, surprise, then something that looked like pain before settling into careful neutrality.

"I should've known you'd be the detective they'd send."

Four years. Four years since he'd last seen her, and she looked the same. Dark hair catching the light. Intelligent blue eyes that missed nothing. A quiet strength beneath delicate features.

The sight of her hit him like a physical blow. When had she come back? How long had she been here?

The officer taking her statement stepped aside, leaving them alone. Silence stretched between them, heavy with things left unsaid.

"I didn't know you were back in town," He finally managed to say.

"I didn't exactly advertise it." Her tone was cool. Controlled. She was building walls and he deserved every one of them.

He sat across from her, notebook in hand, falling back on procedure because it was the only solid ground left. "I know you've already given a statement, but I have a few follow-up questions."

"Okay."

"Tell me about this locket. Do you have it?"

Her hand lifted instinctively to her throat. "I bought a box of old jewelry at an estate sale, and it was mixed in with everything. It's Victorian. From the late 1800s, I believe."

"What makes it special?"

"I don't know." She met his gaze. No hesitation. No evasion. "There's something inside—a small key and what looks like folded paper. They broke in while I was trying to open it."

"Whose estate sale?"

"The Blackwood's. The mansion on Ridge Road."

The name landed like a freezing rain, sending a chill through him.

"Anything else you can remember?" he asked.

She hesitated. "On my way home from the sale, a black SUV nearly ran me off the road. I thought it was just an aggressive driver, but now..."

"You think it might be connected?"

"Maybe. They might have wanted me to crash so they could search my car. What I don't understand is why he was so desperate to find that particular locket."

Blackwood.

Every cop in eastern Tennessee knew the name. Bootlegging. Organized crime rumors, and the eerie legends surrounding Eleanor Blackwood and how she vanished nearly a century ago.

"There are stories," Jack said carefully. "Old ones."

"What kind of stories?"

He studied her expression—interest sharpening beneath fear. The same look that had always worried him.

"We can talk more about that later, I need you to think carefully," he said instead. "Is anyone else following you? Have you had any strange calls or visits?"

"I've only been back two weeks," she said. "I've been focused on the shop."

Two weeks. And he hadn't known.

"Where were you living before that?"

"Nashville. Consulting."

He nodded, jotting it down.

He collected the locket she'd been cradling in her palms and placed it in an evidence bag.

If this had come from the Blackwood estate—if it was tied to Eleanor's disappearance—then Annie had walked straight into something far darker than a break-in.

He glanced at the bruises forming on her arms, anger burning low and steady.

"I'll need you to come in tomorrow for a more detailed statement."

"Can I come in early?" she asked. "I have the grand opening."

"That's fine."

As Jack left the apartment, one thought burned through everything else: This was one story about the Blackwood's he wasn't sure he wanted to hear.

Chapter 2

COLD AIR PRESSED AGAINST Annie's skin the moment she stepped into the Fairview police station. The place looked exactly as she remembered. Gray walls, scuffed floors, the faint smell of disinfectant and burnt coffee. Why had she expected it to be different? As if it bloomed into a high-tech crime lab the second she stopped being a cold case consultant four years ago.

The interview room hadn't changed either. Fluorescent lights buzzed overhead, throwing harsh shadows across the scarred wooden table. Her hand cramped as she finished signing the last page of her statement. She flexed her fingers, wincing.

She'd insisted on writing it out herself instead of letting someone type it. Some things carried too much weight to risk being misunderstood.

Jack studied the pages. "Is that everything you can remember?"

Even after four years, he still noticed details like her handwriting. How carefully she formed each letter. How deliberately she crossed every t and dotted every i.

"Everything." She rotated her wrist. Pain tugged at the bruises circling her skin. "He knew what he was after. No hesitation. No random searching. He went straight for the locket."

"And you're sure you'd never seen him before? Nothing familiar about his voice or the way he moved?"

She shook her head, though something stirred at the edge of her memory. The efficiency of his grip. The way he'd controlled her balance. But fear blurred the details, and adrenaline scattered them further.

"I need to get back to the shop." She pushed up from the metal chair.

"Annie."

His voice stopped her at the door.

She turned.

For a split second, she saw something in his eyes she remembered too well. Concern layered over restraint. The look he used to wear when they worked side by side and she believed she could trust him with anything.

"Be careful," he said. "Lock your doors. And if anything else happens—anything at all—you call me."

"I will."

The words came out softer than she intended. The space between them thinned, fragile and dangerous. She squared her shoulders and left before he could say more.

The drive back to Main Street took only minutes, but she checked her mirrors the entire way. Every car that turned behind her sent a spike through her pulse.

Calm down.

She drew in a breath and let it out slowly. This wasn't a movie. Not a thriller novel. Whoever broke into her shop knew the police stood between them now. They wouldn't be reckless enough to try again so soon.

Yet her nerves refused to stand down.

The shop looked different in daylight. What had felt charming yesterday now felt exposed. Too many windows. Too many angles. Too many places for someone to watch.

She parked in the alley, keys already threaded between her fingers. The lock turned smoothly. She stepped inside and slid the deadbolt closed.

The shop still looked exactly as she had left it when the police finally cleared the scene in the early hours of morning. Nothing had been touched. Nothing restored. The intruder's presence clung to every corner like a stain that refused to lift.

Overturned boxes lay where they had been dropped. Papers were scattered across the floor in careless drifts. Drawers gaped open. Furniture stood crooked and displaced, pulled away from walls as if the space itself had been searched and violated.

Insurance could replace broken objects. It could not repair the feeling that someone had walked through her life without permission. Someone had entered her space. Her future. Her fresh start—and torn through it with deliberate hands.

Her grand opening was three days away. Three days to put everything back where it belonged. Three days to erase the visible damage before customers ever crossed the threshold.

They wouldn't care about fear or sleeplessness or the bruises still blooming beneath her sleeves. They would come looking for beauty. For history. For stories polished smooth by time. And somehow, no matter what it cost her, she intended to give them exactly that.

She climbed the narrow stairs toward her apartment, planning each step of the morning. Change clothes. Coffee. Start reclaiming control.

The apartment door stood open, and cold flooded her veins at the sight. She definitely remembered locking it. Her hand drifted instinctively toward her phone as a sound met her from inside—a low, broken groan that didn't belong in an empty room.

"Uncle Eric?" she whispered, pushing the door open wider. He was the only other person who had a key. The apartment lay in ruins just like the shop downstairs. Cushions were split open, their stuffing scattered across the floor like snow. Books had been torn from shelves and flung aside. Cabinets gaped, and shattered dishes littered the linoleum. The violence of it stole the air from her lungs as she stepped inside, knowing before she fully understood what she was seeing that whatever had happened here had not been about theft.

And in the center of it—

"Uncle Eric!"

He lay face-down, unmoving. Blood matted his gray hair and pooled beneath his head. His shirt tore open across his back, soaked dark.

Annie dropped to her knees beside him.

"No. Please. No." Her hands hovered, afraid to touch him, afraid not to.

His chest lifted. Fell. Shallow. Uneven.

"Uncle Eric, can you hear me?" She pressed her fingers gently to his shoulder.

His eyes fluttered. Struggled. Focused.

"Annie."

"I'm here. Don't move. I'm calling for help." Her hands shook as she dialed, but her voice stayed steady as she gave the address. Ambulance. Police. Both on the way.

Eric's fingers closed around hers.

"They know," he whispered.

"Who knows? Knows about what? Who did this to you?"

"They know about... about the locket." His breath rattled. "Have to... have to bury it. Too dangerous."

"You're not making sense." Panic tightened her chest. "Just breathe. Please."

His eyes rolled back and his breathing hitched, a thin, broken sound that sliced straight through her. Annie dropped beside him, pressing her ear to his chest, listening for the fragile rhythm of a heart that beat too weakly, too slowly, as if it might simply decide to stop.

Panic clawed up her throat. How did he know about the locket? The question barely formed before her hand moved on instinct, tapping Jacks name in her contacts list.

The screen lit her shaking fingers, and there—like a ghost from a life she'd never truly left—Jack's name glowed back at her. Over the last four years, she could never bring herself to delete his number. "Calloway."

"Jack, it's Annie. Someone attacked Uncle Eric. He's hurt. Bad. We're at my apartment. The ambulance is coming, but—"

"I'm on my way."

The call ended. Four words. Solid. Certain. Her chest loosened around them, and the fact that it made something warm in her gut. She hated that his voice could still melt her. Hated that it still steadied her when everything else was breaking. Hated that after four years—after the silence, the unanswered why, the way he had walked out of her life and left her to stitch herself back together alone—he was still the first person she reached for when blood and terror shattered her world.

Hate would not hold her walls—not when someone had already crossed them, not when the danger had only begun. Heavy footsteps thundered up the stairs as paramedics rushed past her, their urgent voices filling the apartment while equipment clattered against the floor.

As they worked over Eric, Annie's gaze drifted numbly toward the kitchen wall, where something jagged had torn through the paint and caught the light. Letters. Deep and violent. Carved with enough force to scar plaster.

YOU'RE NEXT.

***

Jack had been in the apartment when the EMTs arrived, their boots thudding through the wreckage as they dropped equipment beside Eric's broken body and went to work. Now he took the hospital stairs two at a time, his radio snapping with updates from the crime scene unit still combing through what was left of Annie's home.

Forced entry through a rear window.

Signs of a violent struggle.

Blood consistent with blunt-force trauma.

But Jack already knew what they would find. He had seen the apartment before they rushed Eric out on a gurney. This hadn't been a burglary. Nothing had been systematically taken. Drawers hadn't been emptied—they'd been ripped out. Furniture hadn't been searched—it had been overturned.

Whoever had done this hadn't been looking for property. They had been looking for answers. The wrecked apartment. The deliberate brutality against an elderly man. The warning carved into the wall. Someone was desperate to get their hands on that locket and would do whatever it took to get it.

He should have taken it into evidence immediately. Should have insisted Annie stay somewhere safe. Should have recognized the danger the moment she spoke the Blackwood name.

Eleanor Blackwood.

The case had gathered dust for nearly a century. Annie's purchase had disturbed it. Whatever secrets lay buried there no longer felt secure.

Jack pushed into the surgical waiting area and found her at once.

Annie sat rigid in a plastic chair, hands stained with drying blood, eyes fixed on nothing. Eric's blood.

The sight hollowed his chest.

"Any word?" He dropped into the chair beside her.

"Concussion. Possible skull fracture. They're running tests." Her voice held steady, but a faint tremor ran through her hands. "He was conscious when I found him. Not for long."

"Did he say anything?" She turned, and fear slipped through the careful control in her eyes. "He said, 'They know.' And something about burying it. He wasn't making sense."

Cold slid down Jack's spine.

They know about the locket.

What did Eric know about the locket that would make someone nearly kill him over it? Were they trying to get some information out of him? If so, how long had he kept this secret?

"Jack." She studied him. "This isn't just about the locket, is it? You know more than you're telling me."

He didn't want to frighten her. He didn't want to burden her with shadows and half-buried histories. But he wouldn't hide what he knew—not from her, not now.

"I don't know. But what I do know is the Blackwood's have a long, complicated history here," he said. "Bootlegging. Organized crime rumors. Loads of money and no one is really sure where it came from."

Her eyes sharpened. "And Eleanor?"

"Yeah." He nodded once. "Eleanor Blackwood disappeared back in 1927. All the records say she ran away and started a new life because she was having marriage problems and couldn't legally get a divorce. But there are old diaries and journals and stuff in the library archives that say she never would've left her children. The police searched for months but never found her."

"You think she was murdered?" Jack held her gaze.

"I have no idea, but it makes more sense than her just up and leaving town."

"Yeah." He drew a slow breath. "The locket you found belonged to Eleanor. She supposedly wore it everywhere. How is it still here in Fairview? Wouldn't she have taken it with her?"

Her breath caught.

Silence stretched as Annie stared at the floor, rubbing her lower lip, her mind already moving. He recognized the signs—the way she sorted fear into questions, emotion into patterns.

"What I don't understand," he said, "is why they sold it at all. If they knew it was there, why let it go?"

Her head lifted. "Maybe they didn't know. Not until it was gone." Her eyes widened slightly. "What if there are other things? Hidden in what I bought."

This was how they had always worked. One thought opening another. Truth unfolding in careful steps.

"I want to help," she said. "With Eleanor's case."

Fear tightened his chest—not of her curiosity, but of where it would lead. Of what had already followed her home.

"Annie, someone's already willing to hurt people," he said. "If we keep digging—"

"They'll fight harder. I know." She met his eyes. "But they hurt Eric because of me. Because I found something I wasn't supposed to find. I can't walk away from that."

He drew a slow breath, then made the decision he'd been circling since the ambulance doors closed.

"If this stays what it is right now, I can't justify bringing you any further into it," he said. "But this isn't a normal case anymore. Whoever did this targeted a specific historical object, from a specific estate, tied to a disappearance that was never solved. That makes your expertise relevant—legitimately relevant."

She stilled. "What are you saying?"

"I'm saying I'm not keeping you on the outside." He lowered his voice. "I'm bringing this to my captain and to the task force. I'll request you as a civilian consultant. Officially. Limited scope. Artifact history. Provenance. Estate dispersal. Anything tied to what came out of that Blackwood sale."

Her eyes searched his. "You'd do that?"

"I already called it in from the stairwell." His mouth curved faintly. "They agreed we're past the point of pretending this is a routine assault."

The weight in her shoulders shifted, not gone, but redistributed—fear edged now with something steadier.

"If we do this," he continued, "we do it carefully. You don't go anywhere alone. You don't confront anyone. You document everything. And if I tell you something is too dangerous, you listen."

"Deal."

She held out her hand. He took it. Warm. Familiar. Steadying in a way that unsettled him.

Memory pressed close—late nights, quiet prayers, lines he'd tried too hard not to cross.

He released her hand gently. Those days were behind them. This wasn't about what they had been.

This was about protecting her now. And uncovering whatever someone believed the Blackwoods had hidden well enough to nearly kill for.

Chapter 3

THE AFTERNOON SUNLIGHT POURED through the front windows of Annie's Antiques, turning dust motes into drifting gold and throwing long shadows across the chaos that had once been her carefully staged displays. Annie paused just inside the doorway and forced herself to take it in with fresh eyes.

Overturned chairs. A toppled side table. A display case shifted inches off center, like the shop itself had flinched.

After seeing Uncle Eric's blood on her kitchen floor, this damage should have felt small. It did—and it didn't. The mess looked like a stranger's hands had been everywhere, touching what wasn't theirs, rearranging her life with careless force.

Jack stepped in behind her, the door closing with a muted thud that seemed too final in the hollowed space. He'd insisted on coming with her after the hospital. He said he wasn't comfortable letting her walk back into this alone, not when someone had already proven they would hurt people to get what they wanted.

He didn't speak at first. He didn't have to. His gaze moved the way it always had when he worked a scene—slow, methodical, cataloging what had been disturbed and what had been left behind. He was wearing the 'Detective face' she used to tease him about.

She let her gaze move where his had, noting the small, telling details—the drawer that had been pulled out and shoved back crooked, the papers that had been rifled through but not scattered, the faint drag marks where boxes had been shifted and then abandoned.

"What are you looking for?" She ask Jack after following his pointed looks for several seconds.

"Nothing. Just making sure there isn't anything the team may have missed."

He turned his attention back to her.

"So, where do we start?" Jack asked.

Annie didn't hesitate. She turned and led him toward the back of the shop, past the damaged display and the overturned chair, to the crates she hadn't yet fully unpacked from the Blackwood estate sale. Several lids were loose now. Packing paper spilled where someone had forced it aside. Items sat out of place, returned without care.

"Here," she said. "Everything I got from the Blackwood estate is in these boxes."

They began pulling items free with care. Jack lifted out photo albums while Annie gathered the bundles of old newspapers and correspondence she had stacked aside for later review. The shop grew quiet except for the soft sounds of paper and leather and the faint tick of the wall clock.

Faces from another century stared up at them—formal portraits, family gatherings, society photographs, Eleanor's image recurring again and again, young, composed, and unsettlingly watchful.

Annie laid the newspapers across the counter, skimming headlines until familiar names surfaced. Blackwood. Fairview. Business expansions. Charity events. And then, months later, the careful phrasing surrounding Eleanor's disappearance.

From a smaller crate, she lifted out several clothbound journals and set them beside the papers. Jack brought the albums over and exhaled slowly.

"This is what they didn't want you reading," he said.

Annie opened the nearest diary, the brittle pages whispering beneath her fingers. "Then this is where we find out why."

And together, they started where Eleanor had left her voice behind.

Jack stood close behind her, solid enough that she could feel his presence without looking back. "Crime scene finished up about an hour ago," he said. "They lifted some prints, but most of them will match yours or Eric's."

She nodded, because if she tried to speak, grief might pour out of her instead.

The hospital had promised Eric was stable. No skull fracture. A serious concussion. They would keep him overnight and call if anything changed.

They always said that.

Her mind kept replaying the moment she'd found him—face-down on her kitchen floor, blood matted in his hair, his breath thin and wrong. Every time she blinked, she saw the gouged letters on the wall again.

YOU'RE NEXT.

Jack shifted, gentle but purposeful. "We need to look for anything tied to Eleanor Blackwood," he said. "If they came back twice, they might want more than the locket. Or they missed something the first time. Either way, we need to find it before they do."

They.

The plural snagged in Annie's chest.

This didn't feel like a desperate thief acting alone. Someone had forced her off the road. Someone had broken into the shop. Someone had ransacked her apartment while she sat at the station and wrote her statement. Someone had carved a warning into her wall.

Someone coordinated this.

Someone watched.

"I'll start with the books," she said, moving toward the stacked boxes she'd brought home from the Blackwood estate sale. "If someone hid something in a hollowed-out spine or between pages—"

"Good." Jack pulled out his phone. "I'm ordering lunch. We'll be here a while."

The bell above the door chimed as he stepped outside.

The moment he left the threshold, the shop's silence changed. It didn't simply quiet—it exposed her. The front windows suddenly felt too wide, too clear, too inviting to anyone who wanted to look in and calculate.

He's just outside, she reminded herself. He'll come right back.

She forced her shoulders down and turned to the boxes.

Work gave her something to hold onto. Not control, exactly—but rhythm. Purpose. The familiar comfort of details.

She opened the first box and lifted a stack of books out carefully, like she handled fragile relics in a museum. Her fingers traced the cracked leather. She breathed in the faint scent of old paper and dust and time.

She flipped through each volume, her thumb skimming page edges, her gaze searching the seams where someone might tuck a note. She checked the inside covers for loose liners, ran a fingernail along the inner spine, pressed gently at the back boards in case she found an unnatural give.

She kept her breathing steady.

She kept her mind from straying back to blood.

A leather-bound copy of Pride and Prejudice from the 1920s. Beautiful. She verified the publisher page, checked for a signature or bookplate, and found none. She set it aside on a shelf she'd already cleared for high-value stock.

A signed copy of The Adventures of Tom Sawyer. She held it up to the light, checking for altered pages or glued inserts, then smiled despite herself at the neat inscription inside.

Normal. Let it be normal.

After ten minutes, she paused and scanned the small pile she'd organized. These books would sell for good money—real money. Enough to pay a month's rent, maybe two. Enough to help keep her shop afloat.

Not enough to justify an attack.

Not enough to explain why a masked man had slammed her against a wall and demanded a locket like his life depended on it.

The locket had done something to this town. To its buried history. To whoever guarded the Blackwoods' secrets.

She slid a copy of Wuthering Heights onto the shelf and shifted her stance as her bruises tugged at her wrists. Pain reminded her she lived in a body, not just in her head. The ache grounded her, and she hated that she needed it.

The bell chimed.

"Took you long enough," Annie called without looking up, relief already loosening her chest. "I thought your sergeant called you back."

"Oh—I'm sorry to bother you." A woman's voice. Not Jack's.

Annie's stomach tightened. She lifted her head.

A well-dressed woman in her forties stood just inside the door with a little girl who couldn't be more than six. The child shifted from foot to foot, knees pressed together, face pinched in urgent misery.

The woman held a handbag that looked too expensive for the town—structured leather, polished hardware, the kind you bought in a department store in Nashville, not a small mountain shop.

"My daughter needs to use the restroom," the woman said, tone pleasant, practiced. "I saw your lights on. Is there any way...?"

Annie hesitated only long enough to assess the child. The girl's distress looked real.

"Of course," Annie said, setting the book down. "Back through that door. First door on the right."

"Thank you so much." The woman's smile flashed bright, but something about it stayed surface-level, like a mask worn too often. "Come on, sweetie."

Annie watched them disappear down the short hall. Then she looked at the front windows again.

Jack stood outside somewhere—he had to. He wouldn't leave her alone. Not after last night. Not after Eric.

She went back to the box, but the woman's presence lingered in Annie's peripheral awareness like an itch. She tried to ignore it and let her hands keep moving. Pages, covers, spines. She checked a slim journal with blank vellum pages and found nothing.

She opened a cracked poetry collection and shook it gently. Nothing fell out. Routine steadied her. Then the hall creaked. Footsteps approached.

The woman emerged with her daughter, who looked relieved enough to float.

"Thank you again," the woman said. She didn't head for the door. She lingered, eyes sweeping the shop—not the way a customer admired antiques, but the way an auditor assessed inventory. Her gaze paused on the boxes. On Annie's laptop. On the open ledger where Annie tracked purchases.

Annie's pulse ticked faster.

"I hope you don't mind me asking," the woman added, "but are you the owner? This shop is adorable."

"Yes." Annie kept her expression friendly. Neutral. "Annie Whitaker."

She extended her hand. The woman clasped it—and squeezed with confidence that didn't match the damsel-in-distress tone from a moment ago. Her grip felt practiced. Firm. Steady.

"Sarah Mitchell," the woman said. "And this is Emma."

"Nice to meet you," Annie said, releasing the handshake.

Sarah's gaze landed on the disarray—overturned furniture, scattered papers, the displaced display case. "I heard you had quite an ordeal last night. A break-in, or something?"

The casual delivery prickled Annie's skin.

News traveled fast in Fairview. It always had. But this felt too exact. Too immediate. Like the woman hadn't simply heard gossip—like she'd heard details.

Annie forced a small laugh. "Kids, probably. Somebody looking for trouble."

Sarah tilted her head, studying Annie as if she weighed the answer. "How awful. People don't respect anything anymore."

Emma tugged at her mother's sleeve. "Can we go now?"

"Of course." Sarah smiled again, then turned her attention back to Annie one last time. "I'm glad you're all right."

She took Emma's hand and walked out.

Annie found herself at the window, watching them cross Main Street. Sarah pulled out her phone almost immediately and began speaking, her free hand punctuating her words with small movements. Not frantic. Not worried. Efficient.

Annie's throat tightened.

Calm down, she told herself. She's talking to her husband. She's making dinner plans. She's normal.

Normal people didn't always behave the way Annie expected. Annie knew that better than anyone. She'd built a career on understanding how people hid what they didn't want seen.

Still, her instincts wouldn't quiet.

She scanned the street until she spotted Jack—leaning against a telephone pole near the corner of the building, phone to his ear.

Relief washed through her so sharply it almost made her dizzy. He stayed close. He kept watch. He didn't abandon her.

She stepped away from the window and forced her hands back into motion. Pages. Spines. Covers. She needed evidence, not fear.

But the shop's sounds had changed. Every creak had edges. Every passing shadow carried weight. Suspicion sank into her muscles and stayed there like a bruise.

This was why she'd walked away four years ago. Not because she couldn't do the work. Because the work never stopped doing her.

The constant vigilance. The way danger made her mistrust every smile. The way trauma rewrote ordinary moments into threats.

She thought about Jack—the way their minds used to click into place together, like gears aligning. She remembered the precision, the breakthroughs, the quiet satisfaction of giving the forgotten dead a voice again.

She also remembered the other part. How safe she'd felt beside him. How unsafe that feeling made her. How his presence had tempted her to let her guard down. She'd survived losing him once. She didn't know if she could survive letting him close again.

Her phone sat on the counter near her ledger. She reached for it without deciding to. Her thumb hovered over Jack's contact.

One call. One sentence. I changed my mind. Take the case. I'll stay out of it.

She could hand this back to him and retreat into her old life of antique auctions, display arrangements, customers who wanted stories that didn't bleed.

Then she saw Eric again in her mind—his eyes fluttering, his hand clutching hers, his whisper scraping out like a warning from a dying man.

"They know."

"They know what? Who?"

And why did it matter enough to hurt him?

Annie lowered the phone and slid it away. She couldn't outrun this. She couldn't shop her way out of danger. Whoever had targeted her already knew her name, her shop, her apartment, her uncle.

Distance wouldn't protect Uncle Eric. Truth might.

She pulled another book from the box—a slim volume of poems with a faded cloth cover. Her fingers ran along the spine.

Then she heard it.

A soft scratching sound. Not the building settling. Not the normal creak of old wood. Not the faint tap of a loose windowpane. Something deliberate.

Something that didn't belong.

The scratching came again—longer. Slower. Like someone dragged a tool along wood. Like fingernails carved lines with intent.

Annie's blood turned to ice.

She angled her head toward the sound. The shop held its breath around her.

The back door.

Her mind flashed to the gouged warning upstairs. Letters cut deep enough to feel like wounds.

YOU'RE NEXT.

The scratching stopped.

Silence filled the space it left, heavier than the sound itself.

Annie snatched up her phone. Her hands shook, but she moved fast. She didn't waste time debating. She didn't second-guess. She ran for the front door.

Jack.

She had to reach Jack.

She burst outside and scanned the street. The telephone pole stood empty.

Panic surged. Heat prickled under her skin.

Where did he go?

She turned in a tight circle, searching faces, cars, corners. She didn't see him on the sidewalk.

Then she spotted him at the end of the alley beside her building, body angled toward the shop's rear entrance. He stood still, shoulders set, gaze locked on the back door like he expected it to bite.

Annie sprinted toward him, lungs burning.

When she reached him, she followed his stare.

The back door held a fresh mark—new scratches gouged into the wood, deliberate and deep. Not random. Not from a stray nail or shifting hinge. A message.

Her stomach dropped.

They came back.

Jack didn't look away from the door when he spoke. "They left something."

Annie's pulse slammed in her ears as the afternoon sun warmed her skin and did nothing to chase the cold out of her bones.

"They left us another message," she whispered, and the words tasted like fear.

***

Jack leaned against the telephone pole between Annie's shop and Red's Diner, phone pressed to his ear, eyes fixed on the front windows of Annie's Antiques. Officer Martinez's update tightened something cold and heavy in his gut.

"Run that by me again," Jack said quietly.

"We canvassed the blocks around the shop," Martinez replied. "Found a witness who saw a dark sedan parked in the alley this morning. Tennessee plates, but they couldn't get the numbers."

Jack shifted his weight, scanning the street. "Any description of the driver?"

"No. But here's what stands out. Mrs. Chen from the flower shop says she's seen that same car several times over the last two weeks. Different times of day. Never stays long."

Surveillance.

Someone had tracked Annie long before last night. Maybe even before the estate sale. This wasn't a reaction. It was preparation.

"Start pulling Blackwood connections," Jack said. "Anyone still local."

Martinez exhaled. "That's where it gets complicated. There are more ties than we thought."

"Give me what you've got."

"Simon Blackwood still owns the Ridge Road property. But there are cousins, in-laws, distant relatives. The Blackwood money filtered through half this town. Some legitimate. Some not." Papers rustled. "The Hayworth's on Elm—Sarah Hayworth's maiden name was Blackwood. The Caldwell's—Marcus Caldwell's grandfather worked Blackwood operations during Prohibition. And there are rumors around the Mitchells. No confirmed family line, but questionable money."

"Mitchell," Jack repeated, writing it down. The name tugged at something he couldn't place. "What kind of rumors?"

"Commercial real estate. Thomas Mitchell owns half of Main Street. Nobody can trace where his original capital came from."

Jack added the note, jaw tight.

Through the window, he saw Annie moving among the boxes, her posture focused, methodical. A woman with a small child approached the shop. Annie let them inside.

"Keep digging," Jack said. "I want financial histories, property transfers, shell businesses. Anything that intersects the Blackwood's."

"Already on it."

The call ended.

Jack studied the street again, mentally laying out lines between families, businesses, inheritances, and influence. A network like this didn't survive for generations without people protecting it.

Which meant Annie didn't just stumble on a piece of jewelry. She'd stepped into a legacy.

His phone vibrated with a text from Red's.

Your order is ready.

As he pushed off the pole, movement caught his attention. The woman and child exited

Annie's shop. The woman pulled out her phone immediately, posture shifting from polite to purposeful.

Jack slowed. Not panic. Not concern. Efficiency.

He watched her walk away before turning his focus back to the building.

Whatever they'd uncovered so far barely skimmed the surface. Someone had watched Annie for weeks. Someone had coordinated timing. Someone had escalated to violence in less than twenty-four hours. That kind of behavior didn't come from desperation. It came from fear of exposure.

Jack headed toward the diner—and stopped. A faint sound reached him from the alley beside the shop. Scratching. Not metal. Not footsteps. Deliberate contact against wood.

He changed direction instantly, moving fast but controlled. The sound cut off as he reached the corner. Fresh gouges scarred the back door. They were deep. Intentional.

Jack pulled out his phone and began photographing.

He scanned the alley. Nothing. They'd been there seconds earlier while he'd stood ten feet away.

The front door burst open.

"Jack!"

Annie ran toward him, breath shallow, fear plain on her face.

"I heard something at the back," she said. "And then I came out and you were gone and—"

"I'm here." He kept his voice level. Grounded. "You did the right thing."

She followed his gaze to the door. Her shoulders tightened. Her color drained.

"This isn't stopping," she said quietly.

"No." He kept his attention on the alley even as he spoke. "Not until we understand what they want and why."

"Or until I give it back."

The words didn't sound like surrender. They sounded like exhaustion.

"That's not an option," Jack said. "Not yet. Not until we know what we're dealing with."

"They've already hurt people." She gestured toward the door. "They've made their point."

"And they've made a mistake," he said. "They're showing us how afraid they are of what that locket could expose."

She didn't answer.

"You can't stay here alone tonight," Jack continued. "Not after this."

"I'm not leaving." Her voice stayed steady, but her hands trembled. "This is my home. My business. And I don't have anywhere else to go."

"Then I'll stay." He didn't hesitate. "Storage room downstairs. I can monitor both entrances."

"Jack, you don't have to—"

"Yes. I do." He glanced at the street, the rooftops, the alley mouth. "They crossed a line today. You think they'll respect the next one?"

She looked back at the door. At the words carved into it.

Finally, she nodded.

"The storage room gives me clear sightlines," he went on. "I'll notify Martinez. He'll send someone to process this. If anyone comes back, we won't miss it."

"And if they don't?" she asked. "If they change tactics?"

"They want the locket," he said. "They won't destroy it by accident. That gives us leverage."

She studied him for a moment, then gave a small nod. "Then we do this carefully."

"Always."

He texted Martinez their location and the new threat.

When he looked up again, he saw resolve settling into her posture. Not calm. But not panic either.

"That message wasn't just for me," she said. "It was for both of us."

"Yes," he agreed. "And we're not ignoring it."

They walked toward the diner together.

Jack took mental inventory as they moved—sightlines, exits, blind corners. Protection came first. Evidence second. Questions third.

Inside Red's, a white bag waited on the counter.

They carried it back across the street.

They would eat in the shop. They would go through the Blackwood items piece by piece. They would follow the clues where they led. Whatever someone had tried to carve back into silence, Jack intended to bring into the light.

Chapter 4

THE LATE AFTERNOON SUN slanted through the storefront windows of Annie's Antiques, warming her skin as it spilled across the shop. The light softened the jagged edges of the chaos around her—overturned boxes, half-emptied crates, stacks of books waiting to be examined.

The carefully styled displays she'd prepared for the grand opening now cast long, warped shadows across the scattered remnants of the Blackwood estate sale, transforming familiar objects into distorted silhouettes.

She stood in the doorway for a moment and let herself breathe.

After blood and sirens and carved threats, sunlight felt like mercy.

It didn't erase what had happened. It didn't quiet her mind. But it steadied her enough to move again.

She crossed the shop and knelt beside a wooden crate, its slats darkened with age. Inside, books lay stacked in uneven rows, their spines cracked, their pages yellowed, each one a piece of someone else's past. She lifted the first volume out and carried it to the counter, setting it down before opening it carefully.

Her fingers moved with the ease of habit. She checked the inside covers for lifted paper or glued inserts. She ran gentle pressure along the spine, testing for hollow spaces. She turned each page slowly, letting her thumb ride the edges, alert to resistance or weight that didn't belong.

She wasn't browsing. She was searching.

"Anything interesting in there?" Jack asked from across the shop.

He crouched near a low table, a neat line of photograph albums already stacked to one side. He opened each one, examined the contents, then closed it and set it aside before reaching for the next. Methodical. Controlled. He worked the way he always had—like details formed a kind of prayer.

"Mostly first editions and classics," Annie said. "Beautiful pieces, but nothing that screams *family secret.*" She lifted a leather-bound copy of *Jane Eyre* and tilted it so he could see the embossed spine. "Though I'm starting to think the Blackwoods had excellent taste in literature."

"They had the money for it," he replied.

They'd been at this for hours, combing through the estate inventory with the same deliberate rhythm they'd once used in evidence rooms and courthouse basements. No wasted motion. No assumptions left untested. It surprised her how naturally it returned—the unspoken coordination, the way they divided tasks without discussion, the subtle shifts when one of them found something worth a second look.

It didn't feel like returning to an old partnership.

It felt like continuing one.

She worked through another stack. *Little Women. Great Expectations.* A collection of sermons printed in 1912. A slim ledger that turned out to be nothing more than a book club record from the 1940s. She documented each title in her notebook, marking condition and value out of habit, even as she hunted for clues.

"Look at this," Jack said, holding up a photograph.

Annie closed the book she'd been examining and crossed the shop. The image showed a group of people arranged on the wide stone steps of the Blackwood mansion. Men in tailored suits. Women in long dresses and cloche hats. At the center stood a tall, severe-looking man with his hand resting on the shoulder of a young woman who held a toddler on her hip. Another little girl clung to the woman's skirt, half-hidden in the folds of fabric.

"That has to be Thomas and Eleanor," Annie said. "And their daughters."

"1920s," Jack said. "Based on the clothing. The architecture too."

"Eleanor looks so young."

"Twenty-seven when she disappeared."

Annie leaned closer.

Eleanor's face drew her in. Delicate features. Dark, observant eyes. A faint smile that suggested restraint more than joy. The longer Annie studied her, the more she felt the quiet pull of recognition—not familiarity, exactly, but resonance. As if Eleanor had lived a life where silence mattered.

"She's beautiful," Annie murmured. "They look...happy."

"Appearances usually behave," Jack said quietly. "Especially in families with that kind of money."

She glanced at him, catching the weight beneath the words. But he was already returning the photograph to its sleeve.

They resumed their work.

Pages whispered. Boxes shifted. Sunlight crept inch by inch across the floor.

The ordinary sounds of the shop soothed something in her. For minutes at a time, she forgot the alley. The message. The hospital.

"Jack," she said suddenly, pausing over a brittle document. "What first made you doubt Eleanor's disappearance?"

He stopped, considering. "The timeline. And the gaps. But mostly the timing."

She waited.

"She vanished in March of 1927," he said. "Two weeks before her nephew Richard's eighteenth birthday."

"Her nephew?"

"Thomas's sister's son." He set the document down. "According to the family tree, Richard stood next in line if Thomas died without a male heir."

Annie's thoughts aligned. "Eleanor had two daughters."

"And no sons," Jack said. "At least, none recorded."

"If she'd given birth to a boy..."

"Richard would've lost his inheritance."

Annie's stomach tightened. "That's motive."

"Strong motive," Jack said. "Strong enough to kill for."

"You think Richard did it."

"I think someone did," he corrected. "And I think the family spent the next century protecting whoever it was."

Annie turned back to the crate. Her fingers brushed against something heavier than the others.

She froze, then lifted it carefully.

A large volume bound in cracked black leather rested in her hands. The edges had rounded with years of use. The gilt lettering on the spine had almost vanished. The pages shifted under her grip, worn and loose, as if countless hands had turned them.

"Jack," she said. "Come here."

He joined her immediately.

Her breath caught as she opened the cover.

"A family Bible."

The first pages bore dense, slanted handwriting—names, dates, locations. The ink varied from deep brown to pale gray, layered across decades.

"The genealogy," she whispered.

They bent over it together.

"Isaac Blackwood," she read. "Born Bergen, Norway, 1851. Arrived New York..." Her brow furrowed. "He came with his wife and five children."

Jack scanned the entry. "Complete relocation. No safety net. That takes conviction."

"And ambition."

She turned the page. Business ventures appeared alongside births and deaths. Lumber. Shipping. Rail connections. Coal.

Then the entries grew vague.

"They stop naming industries," Annie murmured.

"They didn't need to," Jack said. "Everyone already knew."

She followed the family line forward. Thomas Blackwood—only son among four children. Sole heir.

Then Eleanor.

"Here," Annie said. "Marriage entry."

Thomas Blackwood married Eleanor Hensley, June 15, 1917.

"She was only seventeen," Annie whispered.

Jack's jaw tightened.

Mary, 1921.

Joy, 1923.

Then—

Eleanor Blackwood. Born October 12, 1900. Orphaned age five. Raised by her aunt, Annabelle Hensley. Married Thomas Blackwood. Mother to Mary and Joy. Disappeared March 15, 1927. With child. God rest their souls.

"They wrote 'disappeared,'" Annie said. "Not died."

"Because no one could prove it," Jack replied. He turned a page.

"Richard Mitchell," he read. "Son of Josephine Blackwood."

Annie calculated. "Seventeen. Turning eighteen in five days."

Jack nodded. "Five days after Eleanor vanished."

"If she'd been pregnant with a boy—"

"Richard would've lost everything."

Annie closed the Bible slowly. Her pulse beat in her throat. "Jack...what if Eleanor was carrying a boy?"

"Then Thomas's bloodline would've continued," he said. "But there's no verifiable record. And without a body—"

Unless the locket held proof. The thought formed fully and settled heavy.

She reached into her pocket and touched the velvet pouch. Her gaze drifted back to the photograph and picked it up. Eleanor's dress blurred. The child in her arms. The girl at her side. The locket nestled in fabrics on her chest. The same curve. The same shape.

Annie's breath caught.

"What if this is why?" she whispered. "What if the locket proves something they couldn't afford to let surface?"

Jack followed her gaze. His shoulders squared.

"That would explain everything," he said quietly.

Annie's fingers tightened around the photograph as understanding threaded through her fear. And someone out there believed it still had the power to tear down a legacy built on blood and silence.

***

Jack studied the photograph in Annie's hands, registering the moment her expression shifted from simple curiosity into something far more intent. Her body went still, shoulders subtly tightening as her focus narrowed, the way it always had when she stood on the edge of a realization. He remembered that look from conference rooms and evidence boards, from late nights when a case finally began to speak.

"What is it?" he asked, stepping closer.

"The locket," she said quietly, lifting her finger to the image. "She's wearing it. I'm sure."

She drew the actual locket from her pocket and held it beside the photograph. Even without perfect clarity, the resemblance was unmistakable. The oval shape. The way it sat against Eleanor's chest. The faint suggestion of stones at the front.

Jack leaned in, studying both. "Have we found any other photographs of her?"

"Not yet. But I'd bet she wore this in most of them." Annie's voice dropped. "What if she knew she was in danger?"

The question settled heavily in his chest.

If Eleanor Blackwood had suspected something—if she had hidden proof, names, instructions, or leverage inside that locket—then the necklace wasn't sentimental. It was strategic. Evidence preserved by someone who believed she wouldn't survive to protect it herself.

"Then whatever's inside matters," Jack said. "And not just to history. It matters to whoever's willing to hurt people to get it back."

He straightened slowly, letting his gaze drift across the shop. Boxes lined the walls. Estate items lay spread across tables. Shadows pooled in corners that had once felt harmless.

"I want that locket opened the right way," he continued. "No forcing it. No damage. If Eleanor hid something, she intended it to be found intact."

"I have some tools upstairs that might work." Annie rose, then hesitated. "Jack, something else happened earlier. A woman came in with her daughter. Sarah Mitchell."

The name triggered immediate recognition.

"I know who she is," he said.

Her eyebrows lifted. "You do?"

"I know where the name sits." He held her gaze. "Go on."

"She asked if her little girl could use the bathroom. The child really did seem desperate, but they were back there longer than they should have been." Annie's fingers worked the edge of the photograph. “And she kept looking around. Not browsing. Assessing.”

“You think she was gathering information.”

“I think she wasn’t here for antiques.” Annie inhaled slowly. “And now we find out she’s connected to the Blackwood's.”

“You think she scratched the message into the back door?”

She shook her head. “No. That started after she left. You would’ve seen her go into the alley.”

That matched his memory. Sarah Mitchell had exited calmly, walking east, not toward the back lot. Which meant if she was involved, she wasn’t working alone.

“I’ll check the bathroom,” Annie said, already moving.

Jack watched her navigate the tight path between tables and shelves, aware of how easily blind spots formed in a space like this. He followed moments later.

The bathroom showed no immediate disturbance. Clean. Tidy. Old. Cracks in the tile and faint discolorations spoke to time, not tampering. Then he noticed the small drilled hole in the wall beside the toilet. He crouched, peering through it, catching a sliver of daylight from the alley.

A sightline.

Not dangerous by itself. But useful.

"How long has that hole been there?" he asked when they returned to the front.

"Since I moved in. The previous owner said it was for wiring."

Jack nodded once. "I'll patch it. Today."

She studied him. "You think someone used it."

"I think someone noticed it," he said. "And that's enough."

He pulled out his phone.

"I'm calling Martinez. I want surveillance footage pulled from every street cam on this block going back two weeks, and I want a full background on Sarah Mitchell. Finances. Associates. Family connections. Especially to Richard Henry Mitchell and the Blackwood estate."

When the call connected, he repeated the instructions, then ended it and remained still for a moment, letting the pieces reorder themselves.

A focused theft. Weeks of surveillance. An attack timed while Annie was at the station. A warning carved into her door. And now a building potentially compromised from the inside.

This wasn't random violence.

This was containment.

Someone believed something had escaped their control.

"You can't stay here alone tonight," Jack said.

"Jack—"

"They marked your building while I stood fifty feet away. They attacked Eric in broad daylight. That tells me they're testing boundaries. And escalation only moves one direction."

"This is my home."

"And it's exposed," he replied. "Too many access points. Too many windows. No perimeter control."

"I'm not running."

"I'm not asking you to." His tone stayed even. "I'm adjusting the environment."

She studied him, conflict tightening her mouth.

"Then I stay," he said. "Storage room. I can monitor the front and the alley, and the stairs give me a choke point to your apartment."

"That's not necessary."

"Yes, it is." He met her gaze. "They hurt Eric because of what you found. That means they won't stop at intimidation."

Her phone vibrated.

Jack's followed a second later.

Martinez: Found something. Sarah Mitchell's great-grandfather was Richard Mitchell. County records confirm he inherited the Blackwood businesses in 1928. Everything.

Jack turned his screen toward Annie.

Her breath caught. "1928. One year after Eleanor disappeared."

"And five days after Richard's eighteenth birthday," Jack said. "Which means Eleanor vanished just in time."

The shop felt suddenly smaller.

"What if her death wasn't just about inheritance," Annie said. "What if it was about preventing exposure?"

Jack nodded slowly. "Then the locket may contain something the family never recovered. And someone alive today believes it can still destroy them."

She drew the locket out again. "Then we open it. Tonight."

"Tonight," he agreed. "But we do it controlled."

He stepped aside to make another call, arranging for a patrol unit to pass hourly, requesting a fire inspection of the building's access points, and quietly flagging the alley for unmarked observation.

When he finished, Annie stood watching him, arms wrapped around herself.

"You're thinking this is bigger than one family," she said.

"I'm thinking the Blackwood name didn't survive this long by accident." He scanned the storefront windows. "Power networks don't dissolve. They go dormant."

Silence stretched between them, weighted with what that implied.

Outside, the sun angled lower, throwing amber light across the shop floor, illuminating floating dust that refused to settle.

"Pack essentials," he said. "Clothes. Documents. Anything you can't afford to lose."

Her jaw tightened. "You think they'll try again."

"I think they already are."

Annie exhaled slowly, then nodded.

As she turned toward the stairs, Jack remained where he was, eyes moving, cataloging exits, sightlines, and shadows. The message on her door replayed in his mind. The timing of Eric's assault. The way surveillance had tightened around her without her noticing.

Someone believed the past was about to surface.

Jack intended to make sure it did—on their terms.

Chapter 5

ANNIE WOKE TO THE smell of smoke. It invaded her lungs before she was fully conscious, harsh and chemical, scraping down her throat and sending her into a violent coughing fit that dragged her out of sleep and into terror. Her eyes flew open, but darkness met her gaze—thick, oppressive darkness—broken only by a thin, pulsing line of orange light seeping beneath her bedroom door.

For half a second, her mind refused to accept what her body already knew.

Then the heat brushed her skin.

Fire.

Her heart slammed so hard against her ribs it hurt as reality crashed into place. The building was burning. Her building. The shop downstairs. Her apartment. Everything she had spent four years rebuilding after loss, after fear, after running—every sacrifice, every long night, every fragile hope—was turning to ash beneath her.

Please, God. No.

She threw back the covers and hit the floor, bare feet slapping against hardwood as she ran for the door. Childhood safety lessons surfaced just before instinct betrayed her, and she yanked her hand back from the knob, already imagining blistered skin. She grabbed the shirt from the chair, wrapped it around her fingers, and twisted.

The knob turned, but the door didn't budge.

She braced her shoulder and shoved. The wood didn't give. Panic surged and she slammed into it again, harder this time, driving all her weight forward.

Nothing.

The door hadn't stuck once in the two weeks she'd lived here. She'd heard somewhere that a wooden door could swell and warp during a fire because of the extreme heat. Was that why it wouldn't budge? Or had someone trapped her in here deliberately.

The police could investigate that later. Right now, she needed to get out of here.

Jack.

The thought struck like lightning, igniting a deeper panic that nearly buckled her knees. He was downstairs. In the storage room. If they had blocked her exit, if they had planned this, then they had planned for him too.

Had they already—

No. She wouldn't go there. Jack was trained. Alert. Capable. He would find a way out. But she needed to worry about herself first.

She spun back into the bedroom and reached for her phone, only to find a dead screen staring back at her from the nightstand. Guilt and frustration stabbed through her. She'd forgotten to plug it in. Forgotten, even after Jack told her to.

The smoke thickened, rolling in slow gray waves across the ceiling before lowering toward her face. Each breath burned. Each second tightened the walls of the room.

She didn't have long. Her gaze went to the dresser.

The locket.

Even as survival screamed at her to get to the window, she dove for the drawer, hands shaking as she wrenched it open. The small velvet pouch lay where she'd left it, warm from the encroaching heat, heavy with the only proof they had managed to uncover. The locket. The tiny key. The folded scrap of paper that had raised more questions than it answered.

If she died tonight, if Jack died, whatever truth Eleanor Blackwood had hidden would vanish with them. Her fingers closed around the pouch just as a violent crack split the air as part of the living room ceiling gave way. Embers showered down beyond her doorway, sparks skittering across the floor. The fire was chewing through the building with terrifying speed.

The window. It was her last hope of escape.

She shoved the pouch into her pajama pocket, grabbed her scarf, and tied it over her mouth and nose. The smoke burned anyway, thick and suffocating, each breath like swallowing ash.

She staggered to the window and shoved it open, gulping as cooler night air rushed against her face. Below, the alley yawned into darkness, three stories down, the distance enough to make her vision blur and her stomach revolt.

Her fear of heights surged violently, old and ingrained, dragging memories with it—the oak tree behind her parents' house, the sickening drop, the snap of bone, the months of nightmares that followed.

But fire pressed at her back.

"I need Your strength," she whispered hoarsely. "I can't do this alone."

Scripture rose unbidden, Uncle Eric's voice steady in her mind, echoing from a hospital room long ago. *Yea, though I walk through the valley of the shadow of death, I will fear no evil, for Thou art with me.*

She tore the sheets from her bed.

The flames crept closer, heat swelling the air as she knotted fabric with shaking hands, testing each connection again and again because her life would depend on what she was making. The rope would not reach the ground. She knew that. But it might get her close enough.

Another sharp crack echoed through the apartment. The bedroom door bowed inward, the wood groaning, smoke forcing itself through the seams.

She looped the sheets around the heavy oak dresser she'd bought at her first estate sale, cinched the knot, and fed the length through the window. The ground waited far below.

Heart pounding, lungs burning, she climbed onto the sill and forced herself to sit.

The height stole her breath. Darkness pressed up from beneath her feet, vast and uncertain, her old terror surging until her hands trembled violently against the cloth.

Don't look down.

But she had to.

She lowered herself over the edge and began to descend.

The sheets cut into her palms almost immediately. Her arms shook under her weight. The smoke poured from the open window above her, heat washing over her back as she eased herself lower, inch by inch, praying with every movement. Sirens reached her ears when she was halfway down.

The sound nearly broke her.

“Ma’am! Can you hear me?”

She lifted her head, tears blurring her vision as she focused on the alley below where figures moved beneath flashing red light.

“I’m Carmen with the Fairview Fire Department,” the woman called. “You’re doing great. Just keep coming down. Focus on my voice.”

Annie clung to that voice, to its calm certainty, to the steady instructions guiding her hands. Her arms burned. Her palms throbbed. Blood slicked the fabric beneath her grip, but she didn’t stop.

“That’s it. You’re almost there. About ten more feet.”

Ten feet might as well have been miles.

“My name’s Annie,” she gasped when Carmen asked.

“Annie, you’re being incredibly brave. We’ve got a safety net ready. Just a little more.”

Strength, she didn't know she still possessed carried her downward until the words finally came.

"Okay. Let go. We've got you."

Letting go defied every instinct screaming through her body. But she trusted the voice. Trusted the hands waiting below. Trusted the God who had carried her this far.

She released the sheets.

The net caught her, knocking the breath from her lungs as she fell into waiting arms. Firefighters steadied her, helped her to her feet, wrapped her in a blanket that barely cut the cold shaking through her.

"Jack," she rasped, clutching Carmen's sleeve. "Detective Calloway's still inside. Storage room at the back. Jack Calloway. Please tell me he's out."

Carmen was already speaking into her radio.

Annie watched them run, heart hammering as guilt crashed over her. This was her fault. The locket. The secrets. Every escalation traced back to her.

Her hand closed over the weight in her pocket. The locket was safe. She prayed Jack was as well.

***

Jack woke already choking.

The burn in his lungs dragged him out of sleep before his eyes fully opened, and instinct drove him upright against the storage room wall as smoke rolled thickly across the ceiling, blurring the bare bulb overhead and carrying with it the unmistakable stench of accelerant and burning wood. Heat pressed down from above in suffocating waves, far too intense and far too sudden to be accidental.

Fire.

The realization hit at the same moment he saw the orange glow bleeding beneath the front door, and his body surged into motion before fear could fully register. He crossed the room in long strides, stopping just short of the metal door when he felt the heat radiating through it.

Blocked.

The fire had been placed to sever his access to the stairwell. To Annie.

He spun and drove his shoulder into the back door, throwing his full weight against it. The impact shuddered through his bones, but the door did not give. He struck it again, then again, anger lending power to each blow, but nothing shifted.

Not warped.

Barricaded.

Someone had sealed it from the outside.

They had planned this.

The thought sent a cold surge of fury through the heat in his veins. This wasn't vandalism or intimidation. This was tactical. Whoever had done this understood space, timing, airflow, and human behavior. They had mapped exits. Anticipated response. Cut off escape.

And Annie was upstairs.

The image rose in his mind with brutal clarity: smoke filling her apartment, flames climbing the walls, her trapped while the fire ate upward through the building. Panic surged through him, sharp enough to blur the edges of his vision, and he forced himself to breathe through it even as the ceiling creaked ominously above him.

He would not lose her. Not again. Not because he underestimated someone willing to kill.

The small ventilation window near the ceiling was his only remaining option, never meant for escape, barely large enough to pass a box through, but it was the only opening left. He dragged a chair beneath it, climbed, and used the metal leg to smash the glass outward. It shattered across the alley, shards cutting into his forearms and shoulders as smoke surged more heavily into the room, but he barely noticed.

The opening was narrow. Too narrow. He measured it anyway.

Then he reached into his pocket and pulled out his phone, his hands shaking now despite his effort to control them.

"911, what's your emergency?"

"This is Detective Jack Calloway, badge four-seven-three-one," he said, forcing steadiness into his voice as smoke clawed into his lungs. "Active structure fire at 438 Main Street. There is a civilian trapped on the second floor. Send everything."

He ended the call as the ceiling above him groaned again, a deeper, more dangerous sound this time, and turned back to the window. The building's structure was failing far too quickly. Whoever had ignited this blaze had used accelerants and multiple points of origin, turning the shop into a chimney and the upper floors into a furnace.

He braced his hands on the jagged metal frame and began forcing himself through.

The opening fought him immediately, biting into muscle and bone as his shoulders wedged and his ribs compressed under the pressure. Glass sliced into his skin. Metal scraped across his chest. Smoke poured past his face in choking gusts. For a terrifying moment, he was stuck, suspended halfway through, unable to go forward or back.

Annie's face filled his mind.

He shoved harder.

Pain flared, bright and blinding, but his body shifted, then slid, and finally tore free as he tumbled into the alley below.

Cold night air hit him like mercy.

He rolled, coughing violently, chest burning as he dragged in breath after breath, then forced himself upright and ran. Sirens were already closing in, red and blue lights splashing across brick and pavement as engines screeched to a stop along Main Street.

He rounded the corner toward the front of the building, desperate to find a ladder, a hose line, any sign that someone had reached her.

And then he saw her.

Wrapped in a blanket. Seated on the rear step of an ambulance. Smoke smudged across her skin. Hair tangled. Hands bandaged.

Alive.

The force of it hit him so hard his steps faltered, relief cutting through him with such intensity that he had to steady himself before moving again. She had escaped. Somehow. Against fire and fear and the very trap meant to kill her.

He crossed the street quickly, weaving through firefighters and police, and reached her just as she looked up.

Her eyes met his.

The fear there hadn't fully faded, but beneath it he saw something else flood in—relief, fragile and unguarded, as though she hadn't quite allowed herself to believe he would appear.

"Thank God," she whispered, her voice raw.

He dropped down in front of her without thinking, ignoring the EMT's protest, grounding himself in the simple fact of her presence. Breathing. Warm. Real.

"Takes more than a little fire to get rid of me," he said quietly, though his hands still shook with adrenaline and smoke.

"How did you get out?"

"Bedsheets," she murmured. "The window."

The image struck him with painful clarity—Annie tying knots with shaking fingers, smoke pouring around her, forcing herself into open air while flames closed in behind her. The realization stirred something fierce and protective deep in his chest.

She'd done that. Alone.

He reached out before he could reconsider, letting his fingers rest lightly against the blanket near her wrist, not pulling her closer, not crossing lines, but anchoring the moment.

"I thought you were..." She stopped.

"I'm here," he said simply.

Her gaze lifted to his, and for an instant the chaos around them receded, leaving only the shared truth of survival between them.

Then she looked past him at the burning shell of her building, and her composure fractured.

"Everything's gone," she whispered. "The shop. My apartment. All of it."

He shifted so he blocked part of the view from her, lowering himself closer so she wouldn't have to raise her voice over the sirens.

"The locket," she said then, barely audible. He saw her hand move to her pocket and understood. Relief and dread collided in his chest.

Before Jack could respond, Annie's phone buzzed.

The sound was sharp in the quiet street. Too loud. Annie stilled, then slowly drew the phone from her pocket.

Jack saw the color drain from her face.

She didn't speak. Just turned the screen toward him.

YOU SHOULDN'T HAVE KEPT IT.

WE'RE CLOSER THAN YOU THINK.

Jack's gaze lifted immediately, sweeping the sidewalk, the parked cars, the reflective glass of the storefront across the street. Anyone. Anywhere.

They were still here. Watching.

Annie's hand trembled around the phone. Her breathing had gone shallow, her shoulders tight as if she were bracing for a blow. Fear wasn't loud in her—it hollowed her, stripping the warmth from her eyes and leaving something dark and exposed behind.

Jack stepped closer, angling his body so he blocked her from the open street without making it obvious. Protective. Tactical. Instinctive.

She looked up at him, eyes dark and stripped of everything familiar.

"Where can I possibly go?"

"My family's ranch. Forty miles north. Remote. Controlled access. We can think there. And I can keep you out of sight."

She hesitated only a moment before nodding. He held out his hand for only a moment before she placed hers into it.

And as her cold fingers curled around his, Jack knew they had crossed something tonight that could not be uncrossed. And whatever secrets Eleanor Blackwood had buried, someone had just proven they were still willing to kill to keep them hidden.

Chapter 6

THE MOUNTAIN ROAD TWISTED through dense pine forest as Jack's truck climbed higher into the Tennessee wilderness, its headlights carving narrow tunnels through the dark. Annie sat wrapped in a borrowed EMT blanket that still carried the faint scent of smoke and antiseptic, her bandaged hands folded tightly in her lap.

Exhaustion pressed on her bones, but sleep refused to come. Every curve in the road made her check the side mirror. Every pair of distant headlights sent unease fluttering through her chest.

Jack had taken a winding route, doubling back twice, cutting across old logging roads before committing to the long climb into the mountains. He hadn't said it outright, but she knew he was checking for a tail.

No one followed them.

That knowledge should have comforted her. It didn't.

"How much farther?" she asked, her voice still rough from smoke and coughing.

"Ten minutes," Jack replied, his eyes never leaving the road. "The ranch sits past the last cell tower. Once we're there, we'll be hard to find."

Hard to find. Not impossible.

Annie nodded, drawing the blanket tighter around her shoulders as the road narrowed and the trees thickened. Darkness crowded closer, broken only by the sweep of their headlights and the occasional reflective marker nailed into a trunk. The world beyond the windshield felt untouched, ancient, and watching.

"Tell me about it," she said, needing the sound of something ordinary. "The ranch."

Jack hesitated, then exhaled slowly. "My grandfather bought the land in the early fifties. Two hundred acres, mostly forest and pasture. My parents kept it after he passed. Cattle. Horses. A few rental cabins for tourists who want to disappear for a while."

"Disappear," Annie murmured.

Jack shot her a glance before returning his focus to the road. "It's quiet. That's the main thing."

Quiet sounded like a luxury she no longer trusted.

They rounded a final bend, and the trees opened into a wide clearing washed in moonlight. The ranch house stood at its center, a broad log structure with a stone chimney and a wraparound porch, its windows glowing warm and gold against the darkness. Beyond it, fencing stretched across rolling pasture that vanished into shadowed forest, and farther still, the dark silhouettes of mountains rose against a starlit sky.

"It's beautiful," Annie said, the words leaving her before she could stop them.

Jack pulled to a stop near the porch. For a moment, he didn't get out. He just sat there, hands resting on the steering wheel, gaze fixed on the house as if bracing himself.

"My parents don't know everything," he said quietly. "They know about the fire. About the threats. They don't know the rest. Not about... us. Not about how complicated this is."

"I won't say anything," Annie replied, though the words carried more weight than she let show.

The screen door opened before either of them moved. A woman stepped onto the porch, tall and composed, gray-brown hair pulled back into a loose tie, worry etched into her features.

"Jack."

Relief transformed her face as she hurried down the steps. She wrapped him in a fierce embrace, her hands gripping the back of his jacket as if making sure he was solid and real. Annie's chest tightened with an ache she hadn't invited.

Jack stepped back and gestured. "Mom, this is Annie Whitaker."

The woman turned, her eyes warm and searching as they took Annie in. "I'm Margaret Calloway. Maggie. I'm very glad you're alive, Annie."

"Thank you for letting me stay," Annie said, suddenly aware of the soot still clinging to her shoes and the faint smell of smoke in her hair.

"Nonsense," Maggie said, already ushering them toward the house. "Anyone Jack brings here is welcome. Come inside. You both look like you've walked out of a nightmare."

Inside, the house wrapped around her like something solid and kind. Wood floors softened by rugs. Lamps casting gentle pools of light. Framed photographs lining the walls—Jack as a boy on a horse, Jack in a graduation cap, Jack between his parents, smiling in a way she'd never seen him smile.

Maggie guided them into the kitchen, where the scent of roast and bread still lingered. "Guest bathroom's upstairs, Annie. Towels are laid out. There are clothes in the dresser that should fit well enough for tonight."

The simple kindness nearly undid her.

Twenty minutes later, Annie stood alone in the bathroom, staring at her reflection. Clean. Changed. Wrapped in borrowed clothes that smelled faintly of lavender and soap. The woman in the mirror looked older than she remembered, eyes too large in a face drawn tight by fear and fatigue.

Her fingers slipped into the pocket of her ruined pajama pants, closing around the soft velvet pouch.

The locket.

The weight of it grounded her, even as it stirred the unease beneath her ribs. Eleanor Blackwood had worn it. Eleanor Blackwood had hidden something. Eleanor Blackwood had been afraid.

Annie went back downstairs.

She found Jack in the kitchen, speaking quietly with his father, who looked up and greeted her with the same steady warmth Maggie had shown. Dinner passed in a blur she barely tasted, her thoughts circling the locket, the fire, her uncle lying in a hospital bed because of something she had carried into her home.

Afterward, Jack led her past the house and toward a workshop behind the garage, its windows glowing white in the dark.

"Dad keeps his precision tools in here," he said as he unlocked the door.

The workshop smelled of sawdust and oil and metal. The workbench stood scarred from years of projects, a magnifying lamp mounted at one end, drawers of tools lining the walls.

Annie placed the velvet pouch on the wood.

For a moment, neither of them touched it.

"I keep thinking about her," Annie said quietly. "About Eleanor. The way she looks in that photograph. Like she was already carrying something no one else could see."

Jack nodded. "Whatever's in there, it frightened her badly enough to hide it where she hoped someone worthy might eventually find it."

Annie loosened the drawstring and tipped the locket into her palm.

The metal gleamed softly under the light.

"If she was afraid," Annie continued, "then what she hid wasn't meant to explain everything. It was meant to survive."

She set it on the bench between them.

"Let's find out what she wanted to outlive her."

***

Jack's hands were steadier than he expected as he worked the thin metal awl into the hidden groove along the edge of the Victorian locket. Years on the force had trained him to remain precise even when adrenaline threatened to sabotage fine motor control, but this felt different from any piece of evidence he had ever handled. This object carried a personal gravity, a sense of proximity to the dead that went beyond professional detachment. Eleanor Blackwood had worn this.

She had hidden something inside it knowing her life might depend on whether the truth survived her. And now Annie stood at his side, close enough that he could feel the warmth of her through the thin cotton of her sweater, close enough that every careful movement of his hands seemed to register in the quiet space between them.

The workshop behind his father's garage hummed softly with fluorescent light and the faint vibration of running power somewhere deeper in the building.

The smell of sawdust and machine oil hung in the air, layered over the lingering smoke that still clung to his clothes no matter how many times he told himself he was safely out of that burning building. He was acutely aware of Annie's presence, of the way she watched his hands, of the way she breathed as though she were afraid that too much movement might shatter whatever fragile balance held this moment together.

"Before we open it," she said quietly, "I need to tell you something. That night four years ago, when I... when I told you how I felt..."

Jack felt the shift immediately. The workshop seemed to shrink, the hum of electricity receding behind the echo of memory. He didn't look up, not yet, because he already knew what he would see in her eyes. He had carried that night with him through every case, every empty apartment, every prayer he almost finished but never quite did.

"Annie, you don't have to—"

"Yes, I do." She met his eyes directly, and the steadiness in her voice forced him to straighten despite himself. "I need you to know that I didn't expect anything from you. I wasn't trying to pressure you or make you uncomfortable. I just... I loved you. And I thought you should know."

The words didn't land softly. They never had. They settled into the familiar ache behind his ribs, the one he'd learned to live around, the one he pretended came from old grief rather than unacknowledged fear.

"I did know," he said finally. "That was the problem."

He didn't give himself time to explain, not because he didn't owe her the truth, but because the truth waited behind too many locked doors, and one fragile piece of antique jewelry already demanded his hands. He bent back over the locket, forcing his focus onto the nearly invisible secondary latch hidden beneath the etched scrollwork.

Victorian craftsmen had excelled at disguising mechanisms, and whoever had made this piece had done so with extraordinary care. The design wasn't ornamental. It was protective.

"There," he murmured when the catch finally yielded. "Got it."

The locket opened with a soft metallic whisper, as though releasing a breath it had been holding for nearly a century. Jack turned it carefully in his palm, studying the contents beneath the magnifying glass. The left chamber held exactly what Annie had glimpsed the night of the break-in—a tiny brass key, ornate enough to suggest it fit something deliberately constructed, not a common lock. But the right side drew his attention immediately.

A scrap of paper, folded until it was no bigger than a postage stamp, lay pressed into the narrow recess. Beneath it, flattened against the gold backing, was a photograph.

"Jack," Annie whispered. "Is that...?"

He eased the photograph free first, using the tip of the awl so he wouldn't damage its fragile edges. It was faded but unmistakable. Eleanor Blackwood stood at the center, younger than he had expected, her dark hair swept back from a face that held neither the calm composure of the family portraits nor the softness of a candid moment.

Three young men stood close beside her, arms linked with each other, their expressions carrying a tension that made Jack's instincts sharpen immediately.

"Richard and his friends," he said. "This must have been taken shortly before Eleanor disappeared."

"Look at their expressions," Annie said. "They don't look like friends. Look at how they're standing."

He saw it now that she'd named it—the stiffness, the way Eleanor leaned subtly away from them, the way her smile failed to reach her eyes. This wasn't camaraderie. It was proximity without consent. Pressure without witnesses.

"What about the paper?" Annie asked.

Jack set the photograph down and unfolded the tiny document with meticulous care. The paper crackled faintly, brittle with age, but the handwriting remained legible.

He read aloud.

"My dearest Thomas..."

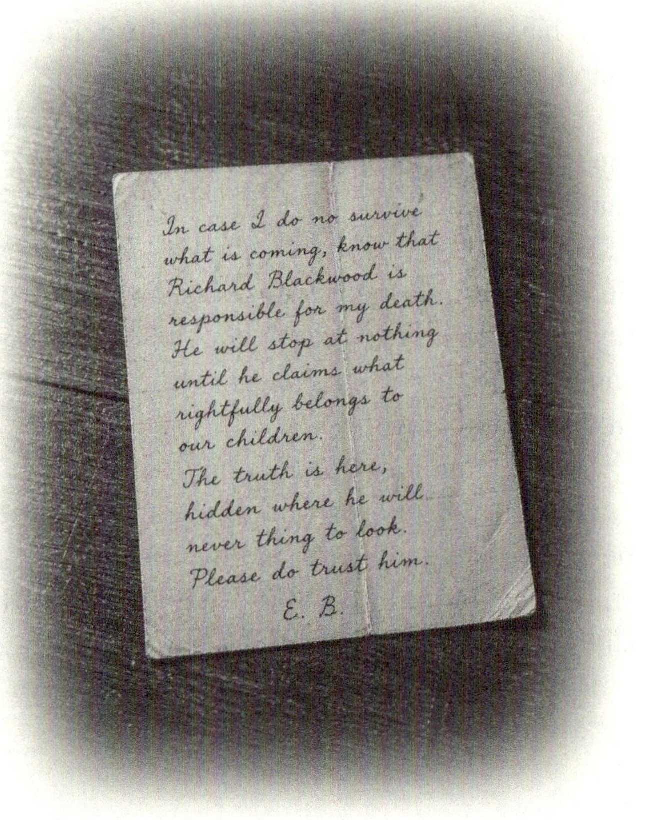

The words pulled the air from the room. Eleanor's voice rose from the page, measured and deliberate, stripped of sentimentality but heavy with foresight.

"She knew," Annie whispered when he finished. "She knew they were going to kill her."

"And she documented everything," Jack said, though the words felt inadequate to the weight of what they held.

A safe-deposit box. A numbered box in a bank that might still exist. Evidence gathered by a woman who had understood, with terrifying clarity, that truth would outlive her only if she concealed it.

Jack folded the letter carefully and replaced it inside the locket along with the photograph and the key, sealing the tiny archive of a life interrupted. "First thing tomorrow," he said, "we contact First National Bank."

Annie sank into the wooden chair beside the workbench, her strength visibly ebbing now that adrenaline no longer held her upright. "Richard really did kill her. For money. For an inheritance that wasn't even his."

"And someone has been protecting that lie ever since," Jack said. "Which means this didn't end with Eleanor. It only went quiet."

She lifted her eyes to him, and something in their dark reflection twisted sharply in his chest. "Joy would be Uncle Eric's grandmother," she said slowly. "Which means he's Eleanor's great-grandson. He's the rightful heir."

"No wonder they wanted him dead," Jack said.

The workshop settled into a heavy silence broken only by the hum of the lights and the distant sound of cattle lowing somewhere beyond the tree line. Jack found himself studying Annie in profile, the same way he used to when they worked late into the night, when she'd lose herself in a theory and forget the world existed beyond the table between them. She had always been this way—drawn toward truth even when it cut, anchored by a quiet courage that didn't announce itself.

"Annie," he said softly.

She turned toward him, and the unspoken years pressed forward between them.

"Jack, I—"

The workshop door burst open.

Robert Calloway stood framed in the doorway, his face drawn tight. "Sorry to interrupt," he said, "but we've got a problem. Maggie just spotted headlights coming up the drive. Two vehicles, moving slow like they're looking for something."

Jack was on his feet before the words finished leaving his father's mouth. "How did they find us?"

"I don't know," Robert said, "but we need to move. Now. There's a trail that leads up to the old hunting cabin. About a mile through the woods. It's defensible."

Jack closed his hand around the locket and reached for Annie without thinking. As they hurried toward the house, he caught the distant gleam of headlights threading through the trees, the slow deliberate movement of hunters who believed their prey cornered.

His parents' sanctuary had been compromised.

And Annie was once again the center of a storm he had no intention of letting reach her.

As they crossed the threshold into the night, Jack felt the weight of the locket in his palm and the warmth of Annie's hand in his. Four years ago, he had convinced himself that distance could protect her. Tonight, running toward the tree line with danger closing in, he knew the truth he had spent so long resisting.

She was never the risk. Losing her was.

Chapter 7

ANNIE'S HEART POUNDED SO hard she could feel it in her throat as she followed Jack and his father through the darkened house. The ranch that had felt so warm and welcoming less than an hour ago had transformed into something tense and watchful, every shadow heavy with threat.

Maggie waited by the back door, a canvas bag slung over her shoulder and a rifle resting easily in her hands, the kind of practiced familiarity that spoke of a woman who hadn't learned survival from fear, but from life.

"I packed some supplies," Maggie said quietly, pressing the bag into Annie's hands. "Food, water, first aid kit, and spare ammunition."

The weight of the bag grounded her, made the danger real in a way the fire and running hadn't fully settled yet. These people barely knew her, yet they were preparing to defend her like family. The guilt pressed hard against her chest.

"I'm so sorry," Annie whispered. "I never meant to bring this to your home."

Maggie reached out and squeezed her arm, firm and steady. "You didn't bring evil here. It finds its own roads. What matters is what we do when it shows up." Her gaze softened. "And we don't turn people away who need shelter."

Through the kitchen window, headlights cut through the darkness of the long drive, moving slowly, deliberately. Two vehicles. Searching.

Robert stepped closer to Jack. "The trail starts behind the barn. It's steep, but it'll take you to the ridge where the old hunting cabin sits. Stone foundation. Only one approach."

"Dad, you and Mom should come with us," Jack said.

Robert shook his head once. "Someone needs to delay them. And this is our land."

Maggie lifted the rifle. "And I intend to stand on it."

Annie's throat tightened. She had lost parents. She had nearly lost her uncle. She could not bear being the reason someone else lost theirs.

"We don't have time," Robert said quietly.

Jack turned to Annie, his hand closing firmly around hers. The contact steadied her more than she expected. "Stay close. We can't use light until we hit the tree line."

They slipped out into the night.

The air was cool, pine-heavy, almost peaceful. It felt wrong that something so beautiful could hold this much danger. They moved quickly across the open ground toward the barn, every instinct screaming exposure. Somewhere behind them, engines cut. Doors slammed.

Voices.

Jack pulled her behind the barn just as flashlights flicked on near the house, beams slicing across the yard in disciplined sweeps. These weren't panicked intruders. They were trained.

"This way," he whispered.

The trail revealed itself only when they were nearly on it, a narrow cut between two massive pines, rising sharply into darkness.

Annie tightened her grip on the strap of the supply bag and followed Jack upward as the ground steepened and the forest closed around them.

Loose stone rolled underfoot. Roots grabbed at her borrowed shoes. More than once, her balance faltered, and each time Jack's hand anchored her without hesitation.

Don't look down.

Don't think about falling.

Think about the next step.

Through breaks in the trees, she could still see the ranch below. Lights moved in coordinated arcs now, sweeping the barn, the house, the tree line.

"How many?" she breathed.

"At least four," Jack murmured. "Maybe more. They're running a search pattern."

The first gunshot cracked through the valley.

Annie felt it in her bones.

Jack stopped, starting to turn back.

"No." She caught his arm. "They knew what they were doing. They chose this. Don't let it be for nothing."

The words surprised her with their strength. Four years ago, fear had dictated everything. Tonight, something else was rising in her—a refusal to be ruled by it.

Jack looked at her, jaw rigid, conflict burning behind his eyes. Another shot echoed. Then silence.

"They're not defenseless," Annie said quietly. "And they're not alone. They have God and home ground."

After a long moment, he nodded once and turned back up the trail.

The climb seemed endless. Her lungs burned. Her legs shook. But eventually the slope softened, and the trees thinned.

The cabin appeared like a dark silhouette against the stars.

It was small, solid, built into the ridge like it belonged there. Stone. Timber. A single narrow approach.

Inside, the air smelled of old wood and dust. A lantern sat on the small table. Jack lit it, and its glow revealed two bunks, a stove, and narrow windows cut to overlook the mountain.

He immediately began checking angles, peering through glass, testing the door, mapping exits.

She saw his training in every movement. She also saw the strain beneath it.

"I'm sorry," she said again, softer now. "For what this is costing your family."

He turned to her. "Stop carrying what doesn't belong to you."

"What if it does?" she asked. "What if Eleanor felt this same weight before she died?"

The words shifted something between them.

Jack studied her, then nodded slowly. "She knew she was in danger. She documented it. That tells me she wasn't just afraid. She was preparing."

"For someone to finish what she started," Annie said.

"And for someone powerful enough to make her disappear," Jack added.

Annie moved to the small table and sat, her fingers brushing the locket through the fabric of her pocket. The object felt heavier up here, as though the mountain itself recognized its presence.

"She wrote about Richard," Annie said. "But she also mentioned someone who tried to warn her. Walter Wainwright. We don't know who he was. Or what he saw. Or whether he survived."

Jack joined her, resting his hands on the edge of the table. "And if there was one, there could have been others. Which means this wasn't just a crime. It may have been a network."

A conspiracy, unspoken but heavy.

Below them, lights still moved faintly through the trees.

"They burned my shop," Annie said quietly. "They barricaded doors. They didn't just want the locket. They wanted silence."

"And they're not done," Jack said.

The words didn't frighten her the way they once would have. They steadied her.

"Then neither am I."

He looked at her sharply.

She met his gaze without flinching. "I spent years letting fear dictate what I deserved. What I was capable of. Eleanor didn't. She wrote the truth even when she knew it might kill her."

Jack's voice softened. "And you climbed out of a burning building to save it."

"Not just the locket," she said. "Her voice."

Something unreadable passed through his eyes.

Below them, the lights began drifting away from the ranch.

"What happens now?" she asked.

"Now we wait," he said. "And tomorrow, we start uncovering what Eleanor died trying to expose."

Annie leaned back against the wall, exhaustion finally settling into her bones. Outside, the mountains stood dark and watchful.

She closed her eyes, one hand resting over the locket, and whispered a prayer of thanks—not for safety, because that was uncertain, but for courage. She was no longer only surviving. She was stepping into the fight.

***

Jack remained at the narrow cabin window, one hand braced against the rough timber frame, his gaze fixed on the dark slope that dropped away toward the ranch below.

From this height, the scattered lights looked deceptively peaceful, as though the night had settled back into its rightful calm. But he knew better.

Twenty minutes of stillness meant nothing. It could mean his parents had convinced their unwanted visitors to leave. It could mean the men in those vehicles were regrouping, repositioning, or waiting for the right moment to strike. The uncertainty coiled tight in his chest, every instinct in him straining toward the darkness.

Behind him, the cabin creaked softly as Annie moved about the small space, checking the supplies his mother had packed and setting them neatly on the table as if order itself could hold back chaos.

The soft sounds of her movements grounded him in a way nothing else could. Even now, with danger pressing in from all sides, he was acutely aware of her presence—of the way the lantern light caught in her hair, of the steadiness in her steps, of the quiet resolve that radiated from her despite everything she had endured in the last twenty-four hours.

The memory of their kiss lingered, not as distraction but as something weightier, something that had settled deep in his bones. It hadn't been reckless or born of fear. It had felt inevitable. But he didn't turn from the window. He couldn't. Someone had to watch the mountain. Someone had to be ready.

"Any movement?" Annie asked quietly as she came to stand beside him.

"Nothing yet," he said, scanning the tree line again. "Either they've pulled back... or they're being smart about it."

She nodded, following his line of sight. "Your parents can handle themselves. I saw your mother earlier. She doesn't strike me as someone who scares easily."

Despite himself, a faint smile tugged at his mouth. "Mom grew up on a farm in eastern Kentucky. Started hunting when she was eight. Dad likes to say she's the better shot. He's probably right."

Annie glanced at him. "How did they meet?"

The question caught him slightly off guard. He shifted his weight, settling into the chair by the window without taking his eyes from the valley. "College. UT. Dad was studying agriculture, Mom was working toward a teaching degree. They met in a literature class. Both of them were the only ones who actually did the reading."

Annie let out a soft laugh, and something in his chest eased. "That sounds exactly like them."

"Dad proposed on graduation day," Jack continued. "Told her he knew she was the one after their first study session. They moved out here almost immediately. The land was mostly wilderness back then. No house. No fences. Nothing but trees and stubborn plans."

"And they built all this," she said quietly.

"They built everything." His voice softened. "They tried for years to have kids. Three miscarriages before I came along. Doctors told them not to expect much. When I finally made it to term, they called me their miracle."

Annie turned fully toward him. "That's a lot to carry."

"It is," he admitted. "They raised me to believe that life is something you guard. That if God gives you a gift, you don't waste it. After Lily..." His jaw tightened. "After Lily, I thought maybe I wasn't cut out for protecting anyone at all."

Annie's fingers brushed his hand. He didn't look down, but he closed his grip around hers.

"And now?" she asked.

Jack exhaled slowly, letting the night air fill his lungs. "Now I think I spent years misunderstanding what strength really is. I thought love was the liability. I thought attachment was what got people killed. But watching you—seeing what you're willing to face, what you're willing to risk for the truth—I think I had it backward."

She waited.

"Love doesn't make people weak," he said quietly. "It's what gives them a reason to stand when everything else tells them to run."

They fell into a silence that felt anything but empty. Outside, a faint mechanical sound drifted up the mountainside.

Jack stiffened, lifting the binoculars from the sill.

Below them, headlights flared to life.

"They're moving," he murmured.

Annie stepped closer, her shoulder brushing his arm as she peered through the glass. "Away from the house."

Jack watched carefully as the vehicles turned onto the winding road and began their descent. He studied the spacing between them, the pace, the deliberate lack of urgency.

"They're leaving," he said, though he didn't allow himself relief. "At least they want us to think they are."

"Do you believe it?"

"I believe they didn't come all this way to walk off empty-handed," he replied. "Which means whatever they're planning, it isn't over."

They stood there until the lights disappeared entirely, until the mountain swallowed every trace of movement. Only then did Jack lower the binoculars.

"We'll give it time," he said. "If they're staging something, they'll get impatient. And if they really are gone, we move carefully. First light."

"And then?" Annie asked.

"Then we go after what Eleanor left behind," Jack said. "We find out exactly what Richard Mitchell and his friends were hiding. And we make sure this ends the right way."

"With the truth," Annie said.

"With justice," he corrected softly.

They turned back into the cabin, the small lantern throwing long shadows across the stone walls. Jack studied her face in the dim light, the quiet courage there, the exhaustion she refused to surrender to. Four years ago, he had walked away from this woman because he had believed distance could protect them both.

Tonight had proven how wrong he'd been.

"Annie," he said, stopping her before she reached the table.

She looked up at him.

"I don't know what happens when this is over," he said. "But I know I'm done pretending that what we share is something I can keep at arm's length. Whatever comes next... I want to face it with you."

Her expression softened, something steady and unafraid settling in her eyes. "Then we're on the same page."

He nodded once. It wasn't a promise of easy days. It wasn't a romantic fantasy. It was a decision.

Outside, the mountains stood silent under the stars. Below them, somewhere in the dark, enemies were retreating—or repositioning. Eleanor Blackwood's secrets were still waiting. His parents were still down there. The danger had not passed.

But for the first time in years, Jack felt anchored rather than haunted.

And whatever was coming next, he would not face it alone.

Chapter 8

JACK STOOD WATCH AT the narrow cabin window, one hand braced against the rough timber frame as his eyes tracked the darkness below.

The ranch lay partially hidden by distance and trees, but the faint scatter of lights still glimmered through the forest like fallen stars.

They hadn't moved in nearly twenty minutes, which could mean his parents had managed to send their unwanted visitors away—or that Something far worse had happened. The uncertainty gnawed at him, tightening his chest with every passing second.

Behind him, the soft sounds of movement carried through the small cabin as Annie shifted supplies, checking and rechecking the bag his mother had pressed into her hands. The scrape of fabric, the quiet clink of metal, the careful way she tried to stay useful instead of still.

He felt her presence even without turning, felt the warmth of her only a few feet away, felt the echo of her mouth against his and the way his world had tilted when she'd kissed him back. Every instinct in him wanted to cross the space, pull her close, anchor himself in the proof that she was real and alive and here.

But he didn't move.

Someone had to keep watch. Someone had to be ready.

And no matter what his heart was doing, the cop in him refused to stand down.

Six years, she'd said. She'd loved him for six years. He had spent four of those years convincing himself that distance was protection, that love was a liability, that caring deeply was the fastest way to put a target on the people who mattered most. But watching Annie tonight and seeing the way she faced danger with quiet resolve, he finally understood how wrong he'd been.

Love wasn't weakness.

Love was what made people stand when fear told them to run.

"Any movement?" Annie asked softly as she joined him at the window.

"Nothing for the past few minutes," he said, scanning the tree line again. "They might have given up for now." He hesitated, then added, "Or they're regrouping."

"Your parents can handle themselves," she said. "Did you see the way your mother held that rifle? She's not someone to underestimate."

Despite the knot in his chest, a faint smile tugged at his mouth. "Mom grew up on a farm in eastern Kentucky. Started hunting when she was eight. Dad likes to joke that she's a better shot than he is."

"How did they meet?"

The question was simple, but the curiosity behind it was not. Annie wasn't just making conversation. She was trying to understand him, the people who had shaped him, the roots beneath the man he'd become.

"College," he said, lowering himself into the chair near the window while keeping his gaze on the valley. "Dad was studying agriculture at UT. Mom was working toward her teaching degree. They met in a literature class—both of them were the only students who actually did the reading."

Her soft laugh cut through the tension, warm and familiar. "That sounds like them."

"Dad proposed on graduation day," Jack continued. "Said he'd known since their first study session that she was the one. They moved out here right after the wedding. The land came from my great-grandfather, but it was mostly wilderness then. They built everything from scratch."

"Including the family."

"Including the family." His voice lowered. "They tried for years to have kids. Mom had three miscarriages before I was born. The doctors told them it probably wouldn't happen."

"But it did."

"But it did. And they never forgot it." He finally turned to Annie. "They always called me their miracle baby. That's a lot to live up to."

Understanding softened her eyes. "Is that why you became a cop? To live up to being their miracle?"

"Maybe," he admitted. "Or maybe I just wanted to protect people the way they protected me." He dragged a hand through his hair. "After Lily died, I thought I'd failed at the one thing I was supposed to do."

"And now?"

"Now I think maybe I was meant to protect you." The truth slipped out before he could stop it. "Maybe everything that happened—Memphis, Fairview, even the way I walked away from you—maybe it was all leading here. To you. To this."

Annie reached for his hand, threading her fingers through his.

"Or maybe we were meant to protect each other."

The contact grounded him, warmed him, steadied something that had been unmoored for years. He studied her profile in the lantern glow, the resolve in her expression, the courage that never seemed to dim no matter how brutal the night became.

"Annie," he said quietly. "Earlier... when you asked about the future."

She lifted her gaze.

"I meant it. But I meant something else too." He turned fully toward her. "I meant that I want to spend the rest of my life solving mysteries with you. Not just as your partner. As your husband."

Her breath caught.

"Jack..."

"I know it's fast. I know we're hiding from killers and none of this is normal and—"

"It's not too fast," she interrupted. "We've already lost four years. I'm not losing any more pretending this isn't real."

"So that's a yes?"

"That's a 'ask me again when we're not hiding from killers in a mountain cabin.'" A smile curved her mouth. "But the answer's going to be yes."

Relief flooded him so hard his chest ached. Determination followed close behind. He would finish this. He would keep her alive. He would bring Eleanor Blackwood justice. And then he would spend the rest of his life proving he was done running.

A distant rumble broke through the quiet.

Jack turned back to the window just as headlights began moving down the mountain road.

"They're leaving," he said.

"Think it's a trap?"

"Maybe. But they wouldn't advertise it if they were waiting us out." He watched until the lights vanished. "We'll wait another hour. Then we move."

"And then?"

"Then we go to that bank," he said. "And we find out exactly what Eleanor left behind. And we end this."

As they settled into the quiet again, Jack's thoughts drifted to his parents and the life they'd built on this mountain. Forty years of choosing each other. Forty years of choosing courage over fear.

He wanted that. With Annie.

Eleanor Blackwood had believed someone would one day be brave enough to finish what she started.

Jack intended to make sure she was right.

And he intended to make sure Annie lived to see it.

***

Jack pressed himself flat against the cold stone wall of the cave, every muscle locked as he positioned his body between Annie and the narrow entrance.

The rock leached heat from his skin, but it was the sound of voices above them that made his blood run cold—men close enough that he could hear the scrape of boots on stone, the low edge of impatience in their words.

Still, it was Annie's presence in the darkness beside him that made his pulse race for entirely different reasons. He could feel her there without seeing her, could sense the steady courage in her breathing, the fragile, unbreakable reality that she was alive and in his arms' reach.

I love you, Annie. I've loved you for years.

The words echoed through him, as real and dangerous as the men searching the ridge above. He'd finally spoken the truth he'd carried for four years, words that had burned in his chest every time he'd seen her smile, every time she'd leaned close over a case file, every time he'd forced himself to look away because wanting her had felt like inviting disaster.

Now they were trapped in a cave while armed men hunted them, and he couldn't see her face, couldn't read her expression, couldn't know whether his confession had comforted her or burdened her. The uncertainty clawed at him almost as fiercely as the threat overhead.

"They've got to be close," one of the voices said from somewhere above the cave. "Thomas said they were definitely on this ridge."

Thomas.

Jack filed the name away instantly, locking it into the growing mental board of players and motives. Another piece of the puzzle. Another shadow behind the threat. He didn't recognize the name, but the tone carried weight—someone who issued instructions, someone whose word carried authority.

"Check every crevice, every overhang," the man continued. "They've got something that belongs to our employer, and he wants it back."

Their employer.

The word sent a chill through Jack's chest. These weren't just desperate relatives or reckless vigilantes. These were hired men, working for someone with enough money and reach to organize a coordinated manhunt in the middle of the Tennessee mountains. Someone who knew about Eleanor's locket. Someone who understood what it meant. And someone who was willing to burn buildings, attack civilians, and now execute two people in the dark to keep a century-old secret buried.

Jack's mind raced. Sarah Mitchell had resources. The Mitchell family had legacy money and influence. But was she the architect, or just a piece on someone else's board? Richard Mitchell had murdered for inheritance nearly a hundred years ago—had that instinct for preservation passed down through generations, refined into something colder, more calculated?

A beam of light swept across the mouth of the cave, so close Jack could see dust motes shimmer in its path. He pressed himself deeper into shadow, every nerve tuned to movement. Instinct took over. His arm shifted, angling protectively across Annie's space, blocking the narrow opening with his body.

In the darkness, his hand found hers.

She squeezed back.

The simple pressure sent warmth surging up his arm, grounding him in a way nothing else could. He thought of the cabin, of the way she'd looked at him when he'd spoken about a future he'd been too afraid to claim.

Ask me again when we're not hiding from killers in a mountain cabin. But Jack? The answer's going to be yes.

Hope flared in his chest—dangerous, defiant hope. They had a future. If they lived.

"Nothing here," one of the men called.

The light slid away, vanishing up the rock face, but Jack didn't move. He stayed carved into stone, listening, counting breaths, tracking distance by sound alone. They were lucky—for the moment. But luck was thin cover. The cave was temporary shelter, nothing more. Eventually, they would have to move. And when they did, there would be no stone between them and the men above.

"Jack," Annie whispered.

"Yeah?"

"I love you too."

The words hit him harder than any bullet ever had.

For a moment, the cave, the mountain, the men above them all blurred into nothing. There was only Annie's voice in the dark and the truth she'd just given him. Love. Chosen. Returned. Real.

He wanted to pull her into his arms, to anchor himself in the proof of her heartbeat, to kiss her until the world made sense again. But the murmur of voices overhead tethered him to reality. This wasn't safety. This was survival.

"Annie," he breathed, turning toward her.

"I know this isn't the right time," she whispered. "But I needed you to know. I've loved you for four years, and I'm tired of being afraid of it too."

Her words slid into the hollow spaces his confession had left behind. The same truth. The same long silence finally broken. Something shifted and settled in his chest, not easing the danger, but clarifying it. They weren't just running anymore. They were fighting for something.

"When we get out of this," he said quietly, "when we solve Eleanor's case and bring these people to justice, I'm going to ask you properly. With a ring and everything."

"When we get out of this," Annie corrected, "we're going to solve Eleanor's case together. And then you can ask me properly."

Even here, even now, she was still Annie—unyielding, courageous, refusing to be protected out of her own life. The shape of her strength had always been this way. It was one of the reasons he loved her. It was also the reason he feared for her.

The voices above continued for long, grinding minutes, drifting, circling, occasionally flaring closer before retreating again. Jack tracked them by sound and instinct, counting heartbeats between steps, noting the cadence of boots, the way the search widened. Eventually, the mountain swallowed them.

Silence followed.

Jack waited ten more minutes before risking even a whisper. "I think they've moved on."

"How can you be sure?"

"I can't. But we can't stay here forever." He flicked on his flashlight briefly, shielding the beam as he swept the cave. "There's another way out."

At the back of the cave, the rock folded inward into a narrow black seam—a passage leading deeper into the mountain. He hadn't noticed it at first. He wished he hadn't noticed it now.

"Where does it go?" Annie asked.

"No idea. But my dad always said these mountains are full of old cave systems. The Cherokee used them for centuries."

She was quiet, and he could almost hear her calculating risk the way she always did—measuring danger not against comfort, but against necessity.

"Lead the way," she said.

As he turned toward the narrow opening, Jack felt the weight of everything they'd just spoken settle fully into him. He had spent five years believing love was a liability. A weakness. A death sentence.

But standing in the dark with Annie's hand steady in his, listening to the echo of her courage, he finally understood the truth.

Love wasn't what made people vulnerable.

Love was what made them strong enough to walk into the dark and keep going.

He would keep her alive. He would uncover the truth Eleanor Blackwood had died to protect. And when this was over, he would spend the rest of his life proving to Annie Whitaker that choosing him had never been a mistake.

Even if it meant crawling through every cave in Tennessee to do it.

Chapter 9

ANNIE STOPPED SO ABRUPTLY that Jack nearly collided with her back. Her attention had locked on the sandy cave floor, on the partial impressions stamped into the damp earth—boot prints, unmistakable and recent.

The sight of them sent a cold heaviness sinking straight into her chest. They weren't the first people to discover this underground route. Someone else had already been here. Someone moving through the caves with purpose. Someone who was almost certainly hunting them.

"How fresh do you think those are?" she whispered, though the enclosed chamber made even the smallest sound feel dangerously loud.

Jack crouched beside the tracks, angling his flashlight beam across them with the practiced focus of a detective. He studied the depth, the disturbed grit, the faint dark marks where moisture still clung to the impressions. "The edges are sharp," he said quietly. "And there's runoff where water dripped from their boots. Twenty minutes ahead of us. Maybe thirty."

Twenty minutes wasn't much of a lead, especially not if the people ahead of them knew these caves better than they did. Fear slid through her, familiar and insidious—but this time it didn't settle alone. Beneath it burned something hotter.

She was tired of being hunted. Tired of flinching at every sound. Tired of people being hurt because powerful men had buried a crime instead of answering for it. Eleanor had been murdered nearly a century ago, and even now the truth was still costing innocent people blood and fire.

"Jack," she said quietly, her voice steadier than she felt. "What if we're going about this all wrong?"

He looked up at her. "What do you mean?"

"I mean... what if instead of running from them, we find a way to get ahead of them?" She gestured toward the footprints. "Whoever left those is between us and the exit. If we keep following the obvious route, we're walking straight into a trap."

Jack swept his light along the cave walls, the beam gliding over pale limestone ripples and shadowed pockets in the rock. "These formations usually interconnect," he said. "Multiple chambers, side passages, vertical shafts. But Annie, these systems can run for miles. We could get lost down here."

"And if we don't change course, we could get killed." She pulled the locket from her pocket, feeling its cold weight settle into her palm. "Someone is willing to murder for this. That tells me we're close. Too close for them to be comfortable."

Jack studied her, searching her face. "So what are you suggesting?"

She turned slowly, forcing herself to really look at their surroundings. The air didn't move from one direction alone. There were unseen channels in the rock, faint drafts curling across her skin, whispering of other spaces beyond the darkness.

"We find another route to the surface. We get to a phone. We call for backup. And then we go straight to that bank." She lifted her chin. "Eleanor waited a hundred years for justice. I'm not letting her down because we were afraid to take a risk."

For a long moment, Jack didn't answer. She could almost hear the calculations unfolding behind his eyes—the danger of the unknown weighed against the certainty of an ambush. Finally, he lifted his light and angled it toward the far side of the chamber. “There. That passage slopes upward. It might lead out.”

The opening was narrow, barely more than a jagged seam in the stone, but she could see the incline as clearly as he could. It didn’t plunge deeper. It climbed.

“You sure about this?” he asked quietly.

“No,” Annie said. “But I’m sure about what happens if we don’t try.”

The new passage was immediately more demanding than anything they’d encountered so far. In some places they crawled on hands and knees, the stone scraping against their clothes. In others, the rock narrowed so severely that Annie had to shrug out of the canvas bag and push it ahead of her inch by inch while Jack guided from behind.

The tunnel twisted upward, forcing their bodies into awkward angles. Her arms burned. Her knees ached. Her breath echoed too loudly in her own ears. Still, she noticed the change before Jack said anything.

The air felt different. Lighter.

“I think we’re getting close to the surface,” he murmured when they paused to catch their breath. “Smell that?”

She inhaled and caught it—faint, but unmistakable. Pine. Damp earth. A whisper of smoke. "How much farther?"

"Not much. There's airflow now. That means an opening."

They pressed forward, the passage growing tighter even as hope grew stronger. Annie fought the urge to think about the weight of the mountain above them, about how easily stone could shift and seal them inside a living tomb. Don't think about that. Think about Eleanor. Think about the truth.

But her thoughts betrayed her. They drifted to Jack. To his voice on the mountainside. To the words he'd spoken as bullets split the night air. I love you. I've loved you for years. Four years of believing she hadn't been enough. Four years of rehearsing indifference. Four years of silence built on grief she hadn't understood.

"Light ahead," Jack called.

Relief surged through her.

The passage widened abruptly, and above them she saw it—a faint circle of night, washed pale by starlight. They climbed carefully, using natural holds in the rock, moving slowly so they wouldn't dislodge stone or betray themselves with sound. They were almost there when Annie heard it.

Voices.

Male. Close.

"—should have found them by now."

"They didn't come out the logging road exit. Thomas is sure of that."

Jack froze. So did Annie.

"They're either still in the caves," the voice continued, "or they found another way out."

Jack eased back down, motioning urgently. There wasn't space for them both to retreat easily, and the voices were getting closer. "Check that opening," someone ordered. "Looks like it might connect."

A flashlight beam cut across the mouth of the passage. Annie pressed herself into the rock, heart hammering so hard she was sure it could be heard. The light speared downward, probing the darkness where they hid.

"Too narrow," a man said. "But shine down there anyway."

The beam slid again, sweeping, lingering. Annie shut her eyes and prayed. After a breathless eternity, the light lifted.

"Nothing. Let's check the main trail."

The footsteps retreated. The voices faded. She didn't move. Couldn't. It took several long minutes before Jack touched her shoulder, and only then did she realize she was shaking.

"They're covering all the exits," he whispered. "This is organized. Coordinated."

"How many?"

"At least six. Maybe more." His mouth tightened. "And they're equipped. Radios. Search patterns. Terrain knowledge. This isn't a family cover-up anymore, Annie."

She thought of the voices. The calm. The efficiency. "What if it's not just about Eleanor?" she said slowly. "What if whatever she hid threatens more than just the Mitchell name?"

Jack's gaze sharpened. "Financial crimes. Ongoing operations. Maybe even organized connections that never stopped."

She nodded. "If Eleanor uncovered something that continued through generations..."

"Then we're not just reopening a cold case," he finished. "We're threatening an entire network."

The thought sent a chill through her. And yet beneath it stirred resolve.

"We need to get to that bank," Annie said. "Whatever's in that box, people are willing to kill to protect it. That makes it evidence."

"First we get off this mountain," Jack said. "Alive."

She met his eyes. "And then?"

His expression shifted. Focused. Predatory.

"Then," he said quietly, "we stop running."

***

Jack studied the pale oval of the cave opening above them, committing every contour of stone and shadow to memory while his mind worked through tactical possibilities.

The voices outside had already told him what his eyes could not: these men were organized. Their spacing, their tone, the discipline of their movement through the mountain all spoke of training and coordination. At least six. Possibly more.

They weren't local muscle or desperate relatives scrambling to protect an old family scandal. These were professionals—contractors, security teams, men accustomed to operating in hostile terrain. The kind of men hired when someone had serious money and even more serious secrets.

Under normal circumstances, the smart play would have been to lock down their position, find a way to call for backup, and wait. But nothing about this situation qualified as normal. His parents were somewhere down that mountain, potentially surrounded.

Annie was being hunted through caves like an animal. And somewhere in Fairview, in a bank vault that hadn't been opened in nearly a century, sat evidence that had already driven people to attempted murder, arson, and an armed manhunt.

Sometimes the smart play wasn't the right play.

Sometimes survival demanded offense.

"Tell me about this plan," Annie said quietly.

Jack shifted his weight against the stone, keeping his body angled between her and the narrow entrance. Even now, even knowing she could handle herself, the instinct to shield her rode him hard and relentless.

"They're watching the exits because they think we're trying to escape," he said in a low voice. "They've covered the logging road. They're circling the main cave mouths. They're assuming we'll make a break for the valley."

Annie's gaze lifted to his, alert and intent even in the dim light. "And we're not?"

"We are," he said, "but not the way they expect." He nodded subtly uphill. "They staged vehicles near the old logging station. You don't hike armed teams into terrain like this without transport, communications, and supply support. Those vehicles are their base. Their radios. Their coordination hub."

Understanding sharpened her expression. "You want to take their way out."

"And their way to hunt us." His jaw tightened. "If we strand them up here, blind them, fracture their coordination, we buy ourselves time. Maybe enough to get off this mountain. Maybe enough to figure out who's really running this."

"Jack," she said carefully, "that's incredibly dangerous. If something goes wrong—"

"Something already has," he interrupted quietly. "The moment they tried to burn us alive, this stopped being defensive. They escalate every time we move. Which means we don't win this by staying one step ahead. We win it by breaking their ability to keep coming."

He watched her process that, saw the internal balance shift between caution and resolve. It was one of the things he loved most about her. Annie never rushed blindly into danger, but when the truth demanded risk, she didn't hide from it either.

"What do you need me to do?" she asked.

His chest tightened. This was the part he hated. "Stay here. Keep the locket safe. If I don't come back, you wait until morning, then you find another way down. You get to law enforcement, to the FBI if you have to, and you give them everything."

"Absolutely not." Her voice was calm, but immovable. "We stick together. That was the deal."

"This is different," he said. "This could turn into a firefight. I can't have you exposed—"

"And I can't let you walk into that alone." She stepped closer, lowering her voice. "My chances of surviving this are better with you than without you. And yours are better with me. Besides... you might need a distraction. Or someone to drive. Or someone to make sure you don't bleed out in a ditch."

He searched her face, saw no fear there—only resolve. The same stubborn courage that had made her climb down a burning building on bedsheets and crawl through limestone tunnels without hesitation. Slowly, he exhaled.

"Fine," he said at last. "But if things go bad, you run. You don't look back. You get off this mountain and you get help."

"Agreed."

Jack spent several minutes listening, mapping sound and movement through the stone. The search teams were fanning wider now, voices drifting farther apart, their pattern loosening as confidence grew. He'd counted at least two vehicles staged near the old logging station. That meant fewer men up the slope.

"They left guards with the vehicles," he murmured. "Which means at least two, maybe three men down there. Armed, but not expecting contact from this direction."

Annie's mouth curved grimly. "Because why would anyone be crazy enough to go after them instead of running away?"

"Exactly."

They waited until the voices climbed farther uphill, until the canyon swallowed them into distance. Then Jack eased out of the cave mouth, scanning the tree line, the ridges, the darkness between. When he was satisfied, he offered Annie his hand and helped her out after him.

The forest wrapped around them in cool, resin-scented silence. Stars spilled across the sky in hard brilliance, untouched by any city glow. For a moment, memory tried to intrude—boyhood nights on this same mountain, thinking the greatest danger in the world was getting lost. Now he was stalking armed men with the woman he loved and a century-old murder riding in her pocket.

They moved downhill through timber and rock, using ravines and outcroppings for cover. Jack let old muscle memory take over, guiding them along paths he hadn't walked in decades but still felt etched into bone. He knew where the shale ran loose. He knew where fallen pines created natural barricades. He knew where sound traveled.

"There," Annie whispered.

Lights glimmered through the trees. Two vehicles. A dark SUV and a pickup beside the cracked concrete slab where logging trucks once loaded timber. Cigarette embers glowed as sentries moved slow circuits around them.

Jack crouched, studying the layout, marking distances, angles, blind spots. Not ideal. The approach was exposed, the retreat thin. But the guards' posture told him something important—they were alert, but not expecting a threat from below.

"See that drainage cut?" he murmured. "It runs into the culvert under the pad. I can use it to get close without being seen."

"What about me?"

"You create noise uphill. Not much. Just enough to draw them off the vehicles for half a minute."

He explained the plan carefully, in whispered detail. It was dangerous. There was no dressing that up. But the alternative—waiting to be cornered in caves—was worse.

They synchronized watches, a habit from their detective years, and separated.

Jack remained submerged in the drainage cut as the guards returned to the vehicles, keeping his body pressed into the mud and shadows while their flashlights sliced through the darkness only yards away. He listened as one of them circled the SUV, the beam pausing too long on the ruined tires, then shifting abruptly to the pickup.

"What is that?" a man demanded.

A second voice answered, tighter now. "The tires are destroyed. Both vehicles. Base, we've got a serious problem."

The radio crackled to life almost immediately. "Repeat. What's your status?"

"Staging area's compromised. Vehicles disabled. Unknown contact. Possible hostile presence."

Jack closed his eyes briefly, steadying his breathing as the significance of those words spread through their network. Radios began activating across the mountain, voices overlapping, their once-measured coordination now sharpened by urgency. Their operation was no longer contained. Their control was breaking. He should have felt satisfaction, even triumph.

Instead, unease threaded through him.

Annie should have been back by now.

She should have been signaling from the tree line. She should have been moving toward him, keeping low, following the route they had planned. When another minute passed with no sign of her, tension tightened between his shoulders, every instinct he possessed shifting away from strategy and toward something far more primal.

Then her voice tore through the forest.

"Jack!"

It came from his left, higher on the slope, and it carried a terror so raw it went straight through him.

He surged out of the drainage cut, weapon already in his hand, heart hammering as he pivoted toward the sound. "Annie!"

Silence answered him.

The forest closed in, branches whipping his arms as he ran. His flashlight carved frantic arcs through the undergrowth, illuminating broken twigs, displaced stones, a dropped flashlight lying dark against the leaves. He followed the terrain as much as her voice, reading slope and spacing the way he had learned to do years ago, letting training override panic.

He found the disturbance almost immediately. Scuffed earth. A torn strip of cloth caught on thorns. Then the unmistakable evidence that drove the air from his lungs.

Drag marks.

Fresh. Uneven. Leading downslope into denser timber.

"No," he breathed, the word tearing from him before he could stop it.

He crouched, fingers brushing the ground, cataloging what the forest had already told him. Multiple sets of boots. Purposeful movement. Someone had taken her quickly and efficiently, cutting off the chance for a second call. His chest burned with the force of what he felt, grief and fury colliding so violently he had to still himself or risk losing the precision he needed.

He lifted his head slowly, filtering the night. Somewhere ahead, branches cracked softly. A murmur of voices carried faintly through the trees.

They were still close.

Which meant he was not too late.

Jack rose, every sense narrowing, every scattered instinct hardening into focus. The dynamic had shifted. He was no longer evading pursuit. He was tracking it. The fear that had driven them through fire and stone transformed into something colder and far more dangerous.

They had taken the woman he loved.

And he was coming for her.

Chapter 10

ANNIE PRESSED HER BACK into the rough bark of a massive pine, forcing her breathing to slow even as her heart pounded hard enough to rattle her ribs. The tree towered above her like a sentry, its branches swallowing moonlight and casting the forest floor in shifting patterns of shadow.

Resin and damp earth filled her lungs, grounding her as she peered through the narrow break in the trees toward the logging station below.

The rockslide distraction had worked. She could see the two guards moving away from the vehicles, flashlights sweeping uphill as they investigated the noise she'd created by dislodging stones along the slope. Their attention was exactly where it needed to be.

Now all she had to do was wait for Jack's signal.

She tightened her fingers around the strap of the canvas bag and glanced down at her watch, counting the seconds as they slipped past.

They had done this sort of thing a hundred times in investigations—setups, diversions, controlled movements meant to shift the advantage just long enough to gather evidence or make an arrest. Only this time there were no uniforms coming. No perimeter. No backup on the way.

Only Jack. And her.

Thirty more seconds, she told herself. Just thirty.

She lifted her gaze again—and froze.

A sound had risen behind her that didn't belong to the forest. Not the rustle of a deer or the careless crack of a branch under wandering boots, but something measured. Deliberate. Controlled.

Footsteps.

Annie's pulse thundered in her ears as she slowly shifted her weight, careful not to disturb the pine needles beneath her shoes. She turned her head by degrees, scanning the darkness between the trees. At first, she saw nothing but shadow and layered trunks. Then one shadow moved.

A figure detached from the darkness and advanced directly toward her, not searching, not sweeping the area, but moving with quiet certainty straight for her position, and the realization sent a chill through her—this wasn't a random approach. This wasn't chance. Whoever it was knew exactly where she stood.

She had chosen her route carefully. She had avoided snapping branches, doubled back, stepped where rock met soil. Jack had taught her how to move through terrain without leaving an obvious trail. Yet the figure continued forward with quiet confidence, closing the distance as if following a clear line only she could see.

A memory surfaced with sickening clarity—the small drilled hole in the bathroom wall at her shop, Sarah Mitchell asking to use the restroom, the faint brush of unease she had dismissed as imagination—and the truth slammed into her all at once. They hadn't just found her. They'd been tracking her.

Her breath caught as the truth settled into place. They hadn't needed to search. They'd never lost her. Every place she had gone, every step she had taken since the shop—they had known.

The figure moved into a wash of moonlight. Sarah Mitchell.

She was taller than Annie had remembered, her posture athletic, her stride unhurried. A pistol hung at her side, not raised yet, but present. Ready. Her face held no panic, no desperation. Only focus.

This was not a grieving descendant guarding an old family shame.

This was an operative.

Annie's mind raced, forcing itself to stay sharp. Running blindly would only delay the inevitable. Hiding was pointless if Sarah could track her position. Fighting hand-to-hand against an armed woman trained to hunt was not courage—it was surrender.

Her hands flew to her jacket, her pockets, the strap of the canvas bag. She fought the urge to panic as she searched, fingers sweeping fabric, seams, folds. For one terrifying second she felt nothing.

Her fingertips brushed a rigid edge beneath the lining near her collarbone, and she peeled it free, revealing a thin disk that lay cold and deceptively simple in her palm. It looked like nothing more than a coin, smooth and ordinary—but coins didn't guide killers through the wilderness. Sarah was less than twenty yards away now. Annie could see the faint glint of her weapon. The concentration in her eyes.

There was no more time to consider.

Annie drew her arm back and hurled the tracker downslope toward the logging station with everything she had, praying the sudden shift in location data would send anyone monitoring it in the wrong direction.

Then she turned and ran.

The forest exploded into motion behind her. Branches cracked. Leaves tore. Footsteps surged.

Sarah's voice cut through the night, sharp and precise as she spoke into a radio.

"I have visual on the target. She's moving uphill toward grid four. Cut her off."

The words sent a fresh surge of fear through Annie's chest, but they also snapped something into clarity. They weren't improvising. They were coordinating.

She forced her thoughts to slow even as her legs burned.

Panic gets you killed.

She had seen it too many times in case files. Victims who ran without thinking. Who made themselves predictable. Who exhausted themselves before the real danger ever reached them.

Think like a detective.

Think like Jack.

Jack wouldn't let himself be driven where they wanted him. He would use the land. He would break patterns. He would refuse to become prey.

Annie veered sharply, changing direction and angling back toward the cave system. If she could reach the tunnels, she might vanish into the mountain the way they had before. Stone didn't care about tracking devices. Rock didn't care about radios.

But as she scrambled downslope, her boots slipping on loose shale, a terrible realization struck her.

She was heading straight toward the logging station—toward Jack, toward the sabotage site—and the truth slammed into her with crushing force. If they were tracking her, she wasn't escaping danger. She was delivering it. Her chest constricted as distant flashes of light burst below, followed an instant later by the unmistakable crack of gunfire.

"Jack!" The cry tore from her before she could stop it, echoing across the mountainside.

She staggered as the image formed too clearly in her mind—Jack alone near the vehicles, limited ammunition, no warning.

I led them to him.

The guilt was crushing, immediate, threatening to drop her to her knees.

"No," she whispered fiercely, forcing air into her lungs. "Not happening."

She changed direction again, this time deliberately, recklessly, driving herself downhill. She was no longer trying to escape.

She was trying to intervene.

She tore through the forest, branches whipping her face, roots snagging her feet. Sarah's voice rang behind her, barking coordinates, redirecting unseen teammates. Annie no longer cared about silence or strategy. Only speed.

"Please, Lord," she prayed as her lungs burned. "Please let him still be alive. Please give me time."

The slope steepened, forcing her into a half-slide, half-run. Rocks scattered beneath her weight. Pine needles slicked the earth. The sound of gunfire echoed again, closer now.

She burst from the trees into the clearing.

The sight stopped her cold.

Two men stood near the disabled SUV, their weapons lowered but ready. Between them lay a body.

Even in the fractured light, even from this distance, she recognized the shape of him. The breadth of his shoulders. The fall of his dark jacket.

Jack.

He wasn't moving.

The world seemed to tilt.

For one suspended moment, the forest, the voices, the danger all blurred into irrelevance.

Jack lay motionless on the ground.

And Annie Whitaker refused to let that be the end.

***

Jack lay motionless beside the disabled SUV, his cheek pressed against cold gravel, every breath measured, every muscle locked in restraint. The bullet had torn through his shoulder in a burning line of pain that radiated down his arm and into his chest, but it had missed bone and artery. He knew that much from experience.

What he didn't know was how long he could stay conscious if he kept bleeding like this.

Two sets of boots stopped within arm's reach.

"Check him."

Rough hands rolled him just enough to search his jacket and waistband. They found his service weapon and stripped it away, along with the radio he had taken from the SUV.

He let his head loll, forced his body to go slack, even as agony flared through his shoulder and spots swam at the edges of his vision. He focused on staying still. Staying quiet. Staying alive.

"This is him," one of the men said. "Matches the description."

"Alive or dead?"

"Alive. The employer wants answers."

The word tightened something cold and hard in Jack's chest. Employer. Not client. Not family. Someone was paying for this operation, and paying well enough to field trained teams, specialized equipment, and coordinated search patterns across a mountain range.

"What about the woman?"

"Mitchell's tracking her. She planted the device herself. Should have her within minutes."

Jack's blood chilled. Sarah Mitchell wasn't just connected to this. She was running it.

A beam of light swept the tree line. "Movement. Upslope." The guards turned, weapons lifting, and Jack cracked one eye just in time to see Annie breaking through the trees. She wasn't running away. She was running straight toward him.

A surge of urgency tore through him, sharp enough to override the pain. She must have heard the gunfire. Must have thought he was down. She was walking straight into a kill zone.

"Target acquired," one of the men said into his radio. "Female approaching from sector seven. Moving to intercept."

Both guards shifted position, stepping away from Jack, attention locked uphill.

It was the opening he had been waiting for.

Jack drove his good heel into the gravel and rolled hard behind the SUV just as the men advanced. His hand went straight to his ankle, fingers closing around the grip of the backup revolver they hadn't found. He pushed himself upright, braced his back against the vehicle, and rose.

"Annie, get down!"

The words tore from his throat as he brought the revolver up and fired.

The first shot struck the nearest guard in the chest. The man went down without a sound.

The second guard spun, startled, weapon rising. Jack fired again, but his injured shoulder screamed and the round went wide, chewing into the concrete pad instead. The guard dove behind the pickup, returning fire in a brutal burst that shattered glass and sent sparks ricocheting across metal.

Annie dropped flat behind a concrete barrier as bullets chewed the air above her.

Jack moved, half-falling into cover as the recoil jarred his wounded arm. He forced himself to breathe through the pain, forced his vision to steady, and raised the revolver again.

Three rounds left.

The guard behind the truck had a rifle, cover, and backup closing fast.

"Jack, you're hit!" Annie shouted.

"Shoulder," he called back. "I'm still in it."

Voices echoed from the tree line. Multiple. Organized. Closing distance.

"Team One, converge on base. We have contact."

Jack risked a glance. Dark figures were already moving between the trees above them.

They were being boxed in.

He shifted, pressed tighter to the SUV, and assessed the terrain with the part of his mind that never shut off. To their left, the drainage ditch he had used for approach cut away from the clearing and funneled downhill. Beyond it lay a series of access roads that fed toward the main highway. It was rough terrain, but it was movement. It was escape.

Annie was already reading the same landscape.

"The ditch," she said. "Does it go anywhere?"

"It connects to an old service road. Half a mile down."

"Can we reach it?"

"Under fire?" He grimaced. "Only if we're fast and lucky."

Another burst of gunfire slammed into the SUV, punching holes through the rear panel.

They were out of time.

"On my mark," Jack said. "We move together. Low. Straight for the ditch. No hesitation."

Annie nodded once. Jack counted silently—three, two, one—then fired his third shot, not to hit but to force the guard back. In the same instant, he surged from cover, grabbed Annie's wrist, and pulled her with him as they broke into a sprint. Bullets cracked overhead. Gravel tore up around their feet. Jack felt one punch into the SUV behind them as they dove into the drainage cut and slid hard into mud and shadow.

Jack didn't stop. He hauled Annie after him, boots slipping as they scrambled down the narrow channel, bending low, letting the ditch swallow them.

Above them, voices shouted.

"They went down the run-off!"

"Move! Cut them off!"

The ditch twisted downhill, choked with brush and slick rock. Jack forced his injured arm to work, using his body to shield Annie where the banks narrowed, his breath tearing harshly through his chest as blood soaked his sleeve. The cold water slowed the bleeding, but it also stole strength from his fingers.

They broke from the ditch into a rough cut of trees and old ruts—the abandoned service road.

Jack slowed only long enough to check Annie's face. Dirt streaked her cheek. Her eyes were clear. Focused.

"We keep moving," he said. "No straight lines."

They ran.

Branches whipped their arms. Roots tore at their footing. The forest swallowed sound, but behind them, he could still hear pursuit. Coordinated. Relentless.

And then another sound rose above the forest and the pounding of their own feet—the low, distant growl of engines. Not close, but not far either. More than one. Jack slowed despite himself, lifting his head as he listened, counting by instinct, his unease sharpening with every second. Multiple vehicles were climbing the mountain road. Too many.

The realization made something inside him shift and widen, the situation suddenly feeling larger than the men hunting them through the trees.

Annie heard it too. She looked at him, the question already forming in her eyes. "That's not local response," he said quietly. "And it's not backup."

"Then what is it?"

Jack didn't answer right away. He watched headlights begin to flicker through the trees far below, thin blades of light cutting through the darkness. Reinforcements. Or extraction.

Either way, someone had escalated.

And whoever was directing this operation had just committed far more than mercenaries to silencing Eleanor Blackwood's past.

Jack tightened his grip on Annie's hand.

"Whatever's in that safe deposit box," he said, "it's bigger than we thought."

And the mountain was no longer the only thing closing in.

Chapter 11

THE SOUND OF APPROACHING vehicles grew louder, threading through the trees and up the mountain road in a low, relentless swell. Annie's heart sank as she counted the distinct engine notes. At least four. Maybe more. Too many to be coincidence.

Even if some of them belonged to law enforcement responding to the gunfire, there was no way to know which vehicles carried help—and which carried more of Sarah Mitchell's men.

"We can't wait to find out who's coming," she said, the decision settling in her even as she spoke it. "We move now."

Jack nodded. His face had gone pale beneath the grime and sweat, the blood loss finally beginning to show, but his eyes were still clear, still focused. "The drainage ditch leads to that old access road I mentioned. It's our best shot."

Annie moved to his side and helped him to his feet. He leaned into her harder than he had before, and the motion confirmed what she'd already seen. Dark stains had spread across his shirt despite his efforts to ignore them, the wound in his shoulder bleeding more than he was willing to admit.

"How bad is it really?" she asked quietly as she braced him.

"Bad enough that I'm not going to be much use in a fight," he said. "If we run into more trouble, you're going to have to be the one who gets us out of it."

The words landed heavier than the gunfire echoing through the trees. Jack had always been the one between her and danger, the one who knew what to do, where to move, how to survive. The idea that he was now depending on her to carry them both unsettled her in a way she didn't have time to examine.

"Then I guess it's time for me to return the favor," she said, surprised by the steadiness of her own voice.

They moved under the cover of darkness toward the drainage ditch while the surviving guard continued to fire sporadically from behind the pickup truck. The shots were less controlled now, more desperate, and Annie could hear him shouting into his radio between bursts—calling for backup, for medical aid, for anyone.

The ditch was deeper than she had expected, cut by decades of mountain runoff into a narrow trench that offered welcome concealment. Cold, muddy water surged around their boots almost immediately, soaking through fabric and stealing warmth with ruthless efficiency. Each step became an effort, the slick stones beneath the surface shifting without warning.

"This way," Jack whispered, pointing downstream toward where the ditch disappeared into a concrete culvert. "That pipe runs under the old logging road and ties into the main drainage system."

Annie tightened her grip around his waist and helped guide him forward. The water numbed her ankles and calves, but she barely noticed. Behind them, the gunfire had faded, replaced by shouted commands and the chaotic noise of multiple vehicles arriving at the logging station.

"They're organizing a search," Jack said under his breath, listening. "We've got maybe ten minutes before they figure out which direction we went."

The culvert loomed ahead, a round concrete mouth just wide enough to swallow them. Inside, darkness pressed close and complete. The sound of their movement echoed off the curved walls, magnified until every step and breath seemed too loud, too exposed. Annie had to force down a rising wave of panic as they crouched and entered.

Don't think about the weight of the mountain above you, she told herself. Think about Eleanor. Think about why you're here.

But it was difficult to focus on anything beyond the cold water creeping higher with each step and the sound of Jack's breathing behind her—ragged now, controlled but strained. How much blood had he lost? How long could determination carry him before his body failed him?

"Almost there," he said, though the confidence she was used to hearing had thinned.

The culvert stretched on, a concrete vein running through the mountain's heart. Time lost meaning inside it. Distance blurred. Then gradually Annie felt it—a subtle change in the air. Less stale. Cooler. Moving.

"I see light," she said, and couldn't keep the relief out of her voice.

They emerged onto another drainage pad, this one choked with weeds and cracked by years of neglect. Above it ran the broken line of what had once been a logging access road, the asphalt split and sinking back into the mountain.

"Which way?" she asked as she helped Jack climb free of the ditch.

"Downhill," he said, leaning into her again. "It connects to Highway Nine. About two miles from here."

Two miles might as well have been twenty. Under any other circumstances it would have been an easy walk. Tonight, after the caves and the climb and the blood he was losing, it felt impossible.

One step at a time, she told herself. That was how you survived burning buildings. How you made it down cliffs. How you lived through things that shouldn't be survivable.

They started down the abandoned road, Annie taking as much of his weight as she could manage. The surface was uneven, choked with gravel and roots, but it was still easier than the forest floor. Still easier than the mountain.

"Annie," Jack said after several minutes. "There's something I need to tell you. About Lily."

"Jack, you don't have to—"

"Yes, I do." His voice was weaker now. Each word cost him. "Because if I don't make it off this mountain, I need you to understand why I left. Why I was so afraid."

She wanted to tell him he was going to be fine. That they would make it. That there would be time. But his grip tightened involuntarily around her shoulders, and she felt the tremor she couldn't deny.

"Tell me," she said.

"Lily wasn't just my fiancée. She was my partner. Not officially. But we worked together. Shared cases. Covered each other."

"Like we did."

"Like we did. But deeper. We lived together. Built our whole lives around the work." He stumbled, and Annie tightened her hold. "When she died, it wasn't just losing the woman I loved. It was losing the person who made the world make sense."

"Jack... what happened to her wasn't your fault."

"I know that. In my head. But knowing something and believing it aren't the same." He paused, breath rasping. "After she died, I chased the hardest cases I could find. The most dangerous ones. I thought if I kept everything else from getting close, nothing could take it away."

"Including cold cases."

"Including cold cases. And then you came along. And suddenly I had that again. A partner who saw what I saw. Who understood the work. Who made me better."

Her eyes burned as he spoke.

"And then I realized I was falling for you. And it terrified me. Because I couldn't survive losing another partner. I couldn't survive watching someone else I loved die because of my job."

"So you left first."

"So I left first."

They walked in silence after that, the road curving gently through the trees. Then, around a bend, Annie saw it—the distant glow of headlights. Civilization. Movement. Possibility.

"We're close," she said, hope threading through her exhaustion.

"Annie," Jack said, his voice barely more than breath. "If something happens to me..."

"Nothing's going to happen to you."

"Promise me you'll get Eleanor's evidence to the authorities. Promise me you won't stop."

She felt the weight of him more fully now. Felt the cost of every step.

"I promise," she said. "But we're not finishing this apart. We're finishing it the way we always did."

Together.

***

Jack felt consciousness slipping away in waves, each step down the mountain road requiring more effort than the last. The bullet wound in his shoulder was a constant fire that seemed to be spreading through his entire body, and he could feel Annie supporting more and more of his weight as they made their slow progress toward the highway.

But it wasn't the physical pain that worried him most. It was the growing certainty that he might not live to see this case resolved, might not survive to help Annie bring Eleanor Blackwood's killers to justice.

Or to tell her how much these past few days have meant to me.

Working with Annie again had reminded him of Everything he'd lost when he'd walked away from her four years ago. Not just her brilliant investigative mind or her fearless pursuit of truth, but her compassion, her strength, her ability to see hope even in the darkest circumstances.

She'd risked her life to save him tonight, had charged into gunfire because she'd thought he was in danger. It was the kind of loyalty and courage he'd spent four years convincing himself he didn't deserve.

"Jack, stay with me," Annie said, her voice cutting through the fog of pain and exhaustion. "I can see the highway. We're almost there."

He forced himself to focus on her words, on the sound of distant traffic, on the promise of help and safety just ahead. But with each step, his vision seemed to narrow, and his legs felt less and less willing to support his weight.

"Tell me about the bank," he said, partly to distract himself from the pain and partly because he needed to make sure Annie understood what they were dealing with. "Eleanor's safe deposit box. What's our plan for accessing it?"

"First we get you medical attention," Annie replied firmly. "Then we worry about the bank."

"No." Jack stopped walking, using what remained of his strength to face her directly. "Annie, listen to me. If Sarah Mitchell has the resources to hire professional killers, she probably has connections in the banking industry too. Maybe even access to safe deposit box records."

Annie's eyes widened as she processed the implications. "You think she knows about Eleanor's evidence?"

"I think she's known about it for years, maybe decades. The locket was just the key—the thing that would allow Someone to actually access the box." Jack leaned against a tree beside the road, trying to gather his strength for the final push to the highway. "If we walk into that bank unprepared, we're walking into another trap."

"Then what do you suggest?"

Jack's mind was working slowly, the combination of blood loss and exhaustion making it hard to think clearly. But years of police training and experience with criminal investigations provided a framework for action even when his body was failing.

"We need backup. Official backup, not just local police who might be compromised." He pulled out the radio he'd taken from the mercenaries' vehicle, relieved to find it still functional despite their ordeal. "This frequency connects to their command structure. If we can monitor their communications, we might be able to figure out who else is involved."

"Jack, you need a hospital."

"I need to finish this case." He met her eyes directly, trying to convey the urgency he felt. "Annie, think about everyone who's been hurt because of this secret. Your Uncle Eric, my parents, Ronald Gaines from the newspaper, probably others we don't even know about. How many more people are going to suffer if we don't expose the truth?"

She was quiet for a moment, and Jack could see her weighing his words against her concern for his injury. It was the same analytical process he'd watched her apply to dozens of cold cases, the careful consideration of evidence and options that made her such an effective investigator.

"What if we split the difference?" she said finally. "We get you medical attention, but we also contact federal authorities. FBI, maybe, or the state attorney general's office. Someone with the resources to investigate a criminal conspiracy this large."

It was a reasonable compromise, and Jack felt Some of his tension ease as he realized Annie understood the scope of what they were dealing with. This wasn't just about solving Eleanor Blackwood's murder anymore—it was about exposing a criminal organization that had operated with impunity for nearly a century.

"FBI has a field office in Knoxville," he said. "Agent Sarah Chen—I worked with her on a money laundering case a few years ago. She's honest, competent, and she has the authority to coordinate with local law enforcement."

"Then that's our first call." Annie helped him start walking again, her determination evident in every step. "But Jack, after we make contact with the FBI, you're going to a hospital. No arguments."

"No arguments," he agreed, though privately he wondered if he'd still be conscious by the time they reached the highway.

The lights ahead were getting brighter now, and Jack could make out individual vehicles passing on the main road. Civilization, help, safety—all just a few hundred yards away. But those few hundred yards felt like miles with each step requiring more effort than he had to give.

"Almost there," Annie said, though he could hear the concern in her voice. "Just keep walking. Don't you dare give up on me now."

Give up. The words triggered a memory from four years ago, the night he'd walked away from Annie and convinced himself he was protecting her. He'd given up then, had chosen fear over love, solitude over partnership.

He wasn't going to give up again.

Drawing on reserves of strength he didn't know he still possessed, Jack forced himself to match Annie's pace as they covered the final distance to the highway. Behind them, he could hear the distant sound of vehicles moving on the mountain roads—Sarah Mitchell's people were still hunting, still trying to prevent Eleanor's truth from coming to light.

But they'd underestimated Annie Whitaker. They'd underestimated her courage, her determination, and her refusal to let injustice go unpunished.

As they reached the edge of the highway and Annie began flagging down the first vehicle she saw—a pickup truck driven by an elderly farmer who took one look at Jack's bloody shirt and immediately reached for his cell phone—Jack realized that Eleanor's century-long wait for justice was finally coming to an end.

And this time, he wasn't going to walk away from the woman who'd made it possible.

This time, he was going to fight for the future they both deserved.

Chapter 12

ANNIE SQUIRMED IN THE uncomfortable plastic chair beside Jack's hospital bed, watching the slow, steady rise and fall of his chest. The doctor had assured her the surgery had gone well, that the bullet had missed major arteries and nerves, that he would regain full use of his arm with time. None of that quieted the tightness in her stomach.

Under the harsh fluorescent lights, his skin looked too pale, his lashes too dark against it, his stillness wrong in a way that tugged at something deep and instinctive.

Six hours had passed since the farmer had driven them down the mountain. Six hours since she had called FBI Agent Sarah Chen. Six hours since the night had stopped trying to kill them. And yet Annie could not shake the sense that the danger had only shifted, not ended. Somewhere beyond these walls, Sarah Mitchell was still free. Still calculating. Still moving pieces they could not yet see.

The locket rested in her pocket like a stone, its small weight far heavier than metal should have been. Eleanor Blackwood's voice waited inside it. Her proof. Her century of silence.

Agent Chen had promised she would arrive within the hour, bringing with her the federal authority needed to take this beyond Fairview, beyond influence and old names and quiet favors. Eleanor waited nearly a hundred years for justice, Annie reminded herself. A few more hours should not matter. But they did.

Every minute that passed was another minute for evidence to disappear, for witnesses to be intimidated, for truths to be buried again.

A soft knock broke the stillness.

Agent Sarah Chen stepped into the room, her presence immediately shifting the air. She was in her early forties, her posture relaxed but alert, dark eyes assessing everything in one calm sweep before settling on Annie.

"Ms. Whitaker. I'm Agent Chen. We spoke on the phone."

Annie stood automatically. They shook hands, Chen's grip firm, professional. Her gaze moved to Jack.

"How is he?"

"The surgery went well," Annie said. "He lost a lot of blood, but he's stable."

"Good." Chen nodded once. "I'll need to speak with him when he's awake. For now, I'd like you to walk me through everything, from the beginning."

Annie drew out the locket. Even here, surrounded by medical equipment and security staff, it felt wrong in her palm. Dangerous. She began with the break-in at her shop and did not leave anything out—the attack on Eric, the fire, the chase through the mountains, Eleanor's confession, the safe deposit box.

She spoke steadily, the way she had learned to when the truth needed to be clean, not emotional. Chen listened without interrupting, occasionally clarifying, occasionally making a brief note.

When Annie finished, the room felt smaller.

"You mentioned Mitchell Security Services," Chen said. "We've monitored them for some time. Publicly, they specialize in private recovery and security contracts. Privately, they function as a laundering hub and enforcement arm for clients who prefer problems erased rather than solved."

"So Sarah Mitchell is running a criminal organization," Annie said.

"Sarah Mitchell is maintaining a family enterprise that predates her," Chen replied. "We have long suspected the Mitchell fortune was built through illegal channels. We've never had the documentation to dismantle it." Her gaze sharpened. "If Eleanor Blackwood recorded financial activity, inheritance manipulation, or violence tied to early business interests, it may expose the foundation of that entire structure."

A chill slid through Annie. They had not just uncovered a murder. They had disturbed a legacy.

"What happens now?"

"We obtain a federal warrant for the safe deposit box and coordinate arrests. Quietly, quickly." Chen glanced at Jack. "We also establish protection. Ms. Whitaker will not be left uncovered."

Jack stirred. His eyes opened, unfocused at first, then sharpening.

"What about her safety?" he asked hoarsely.

"Already in motion," Chen said. "Protective detail is being assembled. Your parents are also under guard."

Relief moved through Annie so suddenly her knees weakened.

"When can the box be opened?" Jack asked.

"I'm meeting a federal judge within the hour. If approved, First National will release it under supervision this afternoon."

After Chen left, the room settled again into its low hospital rhythm. Annie remained standing for a moment, looking at Jack, the lines of pain more visible now that his eyes were open.

"You scared me," she said quietly.

"I know."

"When I thought you were—" Her voice faltered. She steadied it. "I realized how little control I actually had over anything."

Jack's hand found hers. His grip was weak, but present.

"Annie... about what I said on the mountain—"

She shook her head. "I understand. Why you left. Why you were afraid." She met his eyes. "But what happened tonight didn't happen because you loved someone. It happened because someone built an empire on secrets."

He was silent, considering that.

"The difference," she continued, "is that this time, you didn't carry it alone."

Something eased in his expression. Not relief. Acceptance.

A knock sounded. Dr. Martinez stepped in, his expression warm.

"Ms. Whitaker, your uncle is awake and asking for you. He's stable. He insists there's something he needs to tell you."

The words hit harder than she expected.

"Can I see him?"

"Of course."

She looked back at Jack. He nodded.

As Annie stepped into the corridor, the hospital sounds closing around her, she felt the strange calm that followed terror—not peace, exactly, but clarity. The violence had not been random. The warning had not been empty. Someone had believed Eleanor's truth powerful enough to kill for.

And now, finally, that truth was no longer buried.

***

Jack watched Annie disappear down the corridor, the quiet click of the door sealing behind her. Only then did he allow himself to sink fully into the pillows, the thin mattress and stiff sheets pressing against muscles that felt bruised far beyond the bullet wound alone.

His shoulder throbbed in a slow, insistent rhythm, pain blooming outward with each heartbeat. The medication dulled the sharpest edges, but it did nothing to ease the weight settling into his bones, or the exhaustion pulling at him from the inside out. Even so, beneath the pain and the haze, something unfamiliar stirred.

For the first time in years, the case no longer felt endless.

Eleanor's evidence existed. Federal authority was now involved. Sarah Mitchell's operation had been named, traced, disrupted. The chain that began in 1927 had finally been pulled into the light. His parents were safe. Uncle Eric was alive. Annie was no longer standing alone inside the storm.

The danger had not vanished, but truth was finally moving, and with it came a fragile, hard-won sense of forward motion.

We're going to make it, he thought. Not because the threat was gone, but because it was no longer hidden.

His phone vibrated in his hand.

Jack frowned, expecting an update from Agent Chen or a message from his parents. Instead, he saw an unfamiliar number and a single line of text.

> The evidence dies with you. Both of you.
> This isn't over.

The room seemed to contract around him as he read it again, then once more, his pulse accelerating. The haze of medication thinned under instinct. This was not bravado. It was not anonymous posturing. The wording was deliberate. Immediate. Close. Whoever had sent it had not done so blindly.

They knew he was awake.

They knew Annie had just left.

Cold slid down his spine as his mind began sorting through the implications. His number was not public. Only medical intake, federal contacts, and law enforcement had accessed it since admission. That narrowed the possibilities to a margin that made his skin prickle.

Hospital security was designed for disorder, not infiltration. Visitor access was fluid. Staff rotated constantly. And Mitchell Security specialized in placing people where they did not belong.

His phone vibrated again.

Room 314. We know exactly where you are.

Jack's blood turned to ice.

They were not watching from a distance. They were inside.

He pressed the call button for the nursing station, keeping his voice low and controlled. "This is Detective Calloway in 314. I need you to contact FBI Agent Sarah Chen immediately. Tell her there is a confirmed security breach and that Annie Whitaker may be in immediate danger. I also need hospital security notified and this floor locked down. Eric Whitaker's room needs protection immediately."

The response was confused, procedural, already too slow.

Jack tore his gaze from the panel and tried to move. The IV lines resisted as he swung his legs over the edge of the bed, the monitors tugging sharply at his skin. Dizziness washed through him, but he braced his good hand against the mattress and forced himself upright.

Hospitals were not safe places. He had learned that early in his career. They were predictable. Accessible. Built on trust. And trust made them dangerous.

He had just started pulling free of the leads when the door opened.

Every instinct in him tightened, muscles coiling despite the injury, his mind already measuring angles, exits, distances. But it was Agent Chen, two federal agents entering behind her, their presence shifting the room from clinical to tactical in an instant.

"We received your message," she said, her eyes moving from his face to the loose IV line, to the phone clenched in his hand. "What happened?"

Jack held the screen out to her.

She read the messages, and he saw the change register in her expression, subtle but unmistakable.

"They're here," Jack said. "Inside the hospital. They knew when Annie left. They knew my room number."

Chen didn't hesitate. "Get him back in bed," she ordered one of her agents. "I want hospital security, state police, and our Knoxville field office notified. Lock this floor down immediately. No movement without clearance."

The room filled with clipped communication, radios coming alive, instructions stacking fast and controlled. Jack allowed himself to be guided back onto the mattress, but his attention never left the doorway.

"Annie went to see her uncle," he said. "She doesn't know."

"She will," Chen replied. "We already have agents moving."

Only then did Jack let out the breath he'd been holding.

As the agents moved to secure the room, his thoughts drifted, unbidden, to Eleanor Blackwood. He was certain she had known this feeling. The moment when threat sharpened from possibility into inevitability.

When silence stopped protecting and started counting down. She had acted anyway. She had written. Hidden. Recorded. She had believed the truth mattered enough to risk her life for it.

Jack closed his eyes briefly, the weight of that settling over him.

They weren't finished. Not yet.

Chapter 13

ANNIE KNOCKED SOFTLY ON Uncle Eric's hospital room door, her heart lifting at the sound of his familiar voice calling her to come in. After Everything that had happened—the attack, the fire, the chase through the mountains—seeing him sitting up in bed with color in his cheeks felt like a miracle.

"Annie, sweetheart." His voice was still hoarse, but his eyes were clear and alert as he reached for her hand. "I've been so worried about you. The nurses told me about the fire, about what you've been through."

"I'm okay, Uncle Eric. We're all okay." She settled into the chair beside his bed, noting the bandages around his head and the way he winced when he moved. "How are you feeling?"

"Like I got hit by a truck, but the doctors say I'll be fine." He squeezed her hand gently. "Annie, there are things I need to tell you. Things about our family, about why those people came after us."

Annie felt her pulse quicken. "What kind of things?"

"I never told you much about your grandmother Joy, did I? About her mother, Eleanor?" Uncle Eric's expression grew distant, as if he were reaching back through decades of memory. "Your grandmother was only four years old when her mother disappeared, but she remembered things. Important things."

"What kind of things?"

"Eleanor used to tell her stories about a special necklace, a locket that contained important papers. Joy thought they were just fairy tales until she grew older and started asking questions about what really happened to her mother."

Uncle Eric shifted carefully in his bed, his eyes never leaving Annie's face. "The official story was that Eleanor ran away, abandoned her family. But Joy never believed it."

Annie's hand moved instinctively to her pocket, where Eleanor's locket rested like a weight of responsibility. "Uncle Eric, I found the locket. It was in the estate sale items from the Blackwood house."

His eyes widened. "You found it? After all these years?"

"There's a letter inside. From Eleanor to her husband. She knew Someone was going to kill her, and she documented Everything." Annie pulled out the locket, watching Uncle Eric's face as recognition dawned.

"Dear God," he breathed. "That's it. That's exactly how Joy described it." He reached out with trembling fingers to touch the tarnished surface. "Annie, do you understand what this means? Eleanor was your great-great-grandmother. You're her direct descendant."

The words hit Annie like a physical blow. All this time, she'd been fighting for justice for a stranger, never realizing she was fighting for her own family. Eleanor's blood ran in her veins. Eleanor's courage, her determination to see the truth preserved despite mortal danger—it was a legacy that had passed down through generations.

"That's why they targeted you specifically," Uncle Eric continued. "Not just because you found the locket, but because you're Eleanor's heir. If there's evidence in that safe deposit box, if there are financial records or property deeds, you would have a legal claim to whatever the Blackwood family left bchind."

"But the Mitchell family inherited Everything when Richard turned eighteen."

"Did they?" Uncle Eric's expression was grim. "Annie, think about this logically. If Eleanor was murdered before she could give birth to a son, if Richard inherited based on a lie, then Everything he gained was obtained through fraud. That kind of inheritance fraud doesn't have a statute of limitations."

Annie felt the room spinning as the implications hit her. The Mitchell family fortune, built over nearly a century on Richard's inheritance of the Blackwood businesses—it could all be illegitimate.

And as Eleanor's descendant, she might have a legal claim to assets worth millions of dollars.

"That's why they've been so desperate to get the locket back," she realized. "It's not just evidence of a murder—it's evidence that could unravel their entire family fortune."

"Exactly. And Annie, there's Something else. Something Joy made me promise to tell you if anything ever happened to her." Uncle Eric's voice dropped to barely above a whisper. "She never trusted banks completely, not after what happened to Eleanor. So she hid things, important family documents, in a place she thought would be safe."

"Where?"

"The old family cemetery, about ten miles north of Fairview. There's a mausoleum there with the Hensley name—Eleanor's maiden name. Joy had a key made to the tomb, and she hid copies of Everything she could find about Eleanor's disappearance."

Annie stared at her uncle, processing this new information. Another hiding place, another cache of evidence that could support Eleanor's claims. "What kind of documents?"

"Letters Eleanor wrote to Joy before she disappeared. Photographs. Even Some financial records that Joy managed to save when the family estate was divided." Uncle Eric gripped her hand more tightly. "Annie, if Eleanor's letter mentions a safe deposit box, and if Joy's documents support her claims, you might have enough evidence to prove not just murder, but inheritance fraud on a massive scale."

The weight of responsibility felt crushing. It wasn't just about solving a cold case anymore—it was about reclaiming her family's legacy, about ensuring that Eleanor's sacrifice hadn't been in vain.

"Uncle Eric, there's Something I need to tell you too. About what we discovered, about who's been trying to kill us." Annie quickly filled him in on Everything that had happened since the fire—the chase through the mountains, Jack's injury, Agent Chen's investigation, the scope of the criminal organization they'd uncovered.

"So Sarah Mitchell is behind all of this?"

"She's part of it, but it's bigger than just her. The FBI thinks the Mitchell family has been using their inherited wealth to fund criminal activities for decades. Money laundering, hired killers, maybe even connections to organized crime."

Uncle Eric was quiet for a long moment, absorbing the magnitude of what they'd discovered. "Your great-great-grandmother was a brave woman, Annie. She knew she was going to die, but she made sure the truth would survive. Now it's up to us to make sure her courage wasn't wasted."

"Agent Chen is getting a warrant for the safe deposit box this afternoon. We're going to open it under federal supervision and see what Eleanor left behind."

"Good. But Annie, be careful. If what I suspect is true, if that box contains evidence of inheritance fraud worth millions of dollars, then Sarah Mitchell and her associates will do anything to prevent it from becoming public."

A commotion in the hallway outside made them both look toward the door. Raised voices, the sound of running feet, what might have been security alarms in the distance.

"What's that about?" Uncle Eric asked, but before Annie could answer, the door to his room burst open.

Agent Chen stood in the doorway, her weapon drawn and her expression tense. "Ms. Whitaker, we need to move you immediately. We have a security breach in the hospital."

"What kind of breach?" Annie was already on her feet, her heart racing.

"Armed individuals on the hospital premises, and we have reason to believe they're targeting both you and Detective Calloway." Agent Chen gestured urgently toward the door. "We're evacuating you to a secure location until we can neutralize the threat."

Annie looked back at Uncle Eric, torn between staying to protect him and following Agent Chen to safety. "What about my uncle?"

"Hospital security is positioning guards outside his room. He'll be safe here." Agent Chen's voice brooked no argument. "But you need to come with me now."

As they hurried down the hospital corridor, Annie could see federal agents at strategic positions, their weapons ready, their eyes scanning for threats. The weight of Eleanor's locket in her pocket felt heavier than ever—a century-old secret that people were still willing to kill for.

I won't let them win, she thought fiercely. *Eleanor trusted the truth to survive, and I'm going to make sure it does.*

But as they reached the elevator that would take them to whatever safety Agent Chen had arranged,

Annie couldn't shake the feeling that they were walking into another trap.

Some secrets she was learning had roots too deep and tendrils too widespread to be easily exposed.

***

Jack forced himself to remain still as Agent Chen's colleague guided him back against the pillows and began reconnecting the monitoring leads he had half-pulled free. Every instinct he had screamed at him to get out of this bed, to get into the corridor, to find Annie.

The threatening messages still burned behind his eyes, not because he feared what they promised for him, but because of what they implied for her. Losing Annie now—after everything they had survived, after finally finding their way back to one another—was a thought he could not make himself face.

"Detective, I need you focused," the agent said, his tone firm but controlled as he adjusted the equipment. "Tell me everything about the messages. When did they come in? Have you seen the number before?"

"First one about ten minutes ago. The second a few minutes after that." Jack handed him the phone. "I don't recognize the number, but the timing means they're tracking us in real time."

The agent studied the screen, then looked back at him. "Any idea how they might have gotten your personal cell?"

Jack closed his eyes briefly, working back through the last forty-eight hours. His number wasn't public. He guarded it carefully. But chaos created openings. "On the mountain," he said slowly. "When we were hiding in the caves, I called 911. If they were monitoring emergency frequencies, they could've traced it."

"Or they have someone inside the hospital," the agent said quietly. "Admissions, records, staff access."

The words slid cold through Jack's chest. Sarah Mitchell didn't just have money. She had infrastructure. Reach. Time. He thought of Annie being admitted, of her name going into a system that dozens of people could touch. "Where is Annie?" he asked.

"Agent Chen is evacuating her to a secure location."

The reassurance didn't land. Jack had seen what Sarah Mitchell's people were willing to do. The fact that they had breached a hospital told him this was no longer intimidation. This was execution.

His phone vibrated again. The agent read the screen, and the tightening of his jaw told Jack enough before he spoke.

"'Room 314. We know exactly where you are.'"

Jack's pulse spiked. "They're here."

The agent was already speaking into his radio, issuing rapid instructions. As he did, the sound rose through the hospital like a gathering storm—raised voices, the clipped echo of boots, the distant keening thread of alarms. Not panic. Movement. Direction.

Another transmission cut through the channel. "We've confirmed multiple armed individuals inside the building. They appear to be conducting a coordinated search."

Jack pushed himself upright despite the tearing protest in his shoulder. "How many?"

"Unknown. But this isn't containment. It's a sweep."

The words settled heavily. This wasn't about silencing one witness anymore. Sarah Mitchell was willing to turn a hospital into a battlefield. Patients. Nurses. Families. All of them leverage.

"What about my parents?" Jack asked. "The ranch."

The agent checked in, listening, then nodded once. "They're secure. No activity reported."

Relief came, sharp and brief, before resolution locked in around it. Annie was being moved. Eric was guarded. But the rest of the building was exposed. "I need out of this bed," Jack said.

"Detective—"

"I'm the one person here who understands how these people operate," Jack cut in. "I've been inside their patterns, their priorities. And this isn't random. This is structured. Which means it has an objective."

Before the agent could respond, another voice broke across the radio. "Confirmed at least six armed individuals. Floor-to-floor progression. They're searching for specific targets."

Specific. The word lodged in Jack's chest. Annie. Eric. Himself.

His phone vibrated again.

This time, the agent angled the screen so he could see it.

> Last chance. Give us the locket, and we'll let the others live.

Jack stared at the message. It wasn't just a threat. It was a negotiation. And negotiations meant uncertainty.

"Can you trace it?" he asked.

"Our tech team is working on it."

Jack nodded, but his attention had already moved past the device in his hand. Somewhere in this hospital, Annie was being moved through hallways under armed protection. Somewhere else, men were advancing room by room. Eleanor's locket was no longer just evidence. It was a trigger point.

He closed his eyes, and Eleanor Blackwood rose in his mind—not as a name in a file, but as a woman who had written, knowing she might not live, who had hidden truth inside a locket because she believed it would outlast her.

She had accepted the cost. And she had trusted someone would finish what she started.

"They don't understand what they're threatening," Jack said quietly. "The locket isn't leverage. It's already a confession. Whatever's in that box is going to surface whether they stop us or not."

The agent watched him carefully.

"She didn't hide the truth, so it could be traded," Jack continued. "She hid it so it could survive."

And he intended to make sure it did.

Chapter 14

JACK GRITTED HIS TEETH as the federal agents helped him transfer from the hospital bed to a wheelchair, every careful movement sending fresh waves of pain through his injured shoulder.

The wound throbbed with a deep, grinding heat that radiated down his arm and into his chest, a reminder that his body had not caught up with the urgency of the situation. The surgeon had been clear—he needed rest, immobility, time. What he was being prepared for now offered none of those things.

But there was no scenario in which he stayed behind while Annie Whitaker walked into danger alone.

"Detective, you don't have to do this," Agent Chen said as one of her agents adjusted the sling, supporting his arm. "We can handle the operation without you."

Jack forced himself to breathe through the pain before answering. "With respect, Agent Chen, you don't know these people the way I do. I've been inside their patterns for days now. I've watched how they move, how they escalate, how they calculate risk." He lifted his eyes to hers. "And I know Annie. I know exactly what she's willing to walk into if she believes it's the right thing to do."

Chen studied him for a moment, as if weighing the cost of arguing against the reality in his voice.

The evacuation route took them through service corridors and freight elevators, far from the public wings of the hospital. Even so, Jack caught fractured glimpses of the chaos they were leaving behind.

Armed hospital security clustered at corridor intersections. Gurneys were being rushed through side halls. A nurse stood pressed against a wall, one hand shaking as she spoke urgently into a phone. This was no longer a containment. It was a crisis.

"How many?" Jack asked quietly as they reached the parking garage.

"Six confirmed injured so far," Chen replied. "Three security guards, two nurses, one physician who was caught between floors."

Jack closed his eyes briefly. Six people whose only mistake had been showing up to work. Six lives pulled into violence because a family had spent a century protecting a lie.

They helped him into the back of an unmarked federal SUV, the seat cool and firm beneath him. Chen took the front passenger seat, already speaking into her radio, absorbing updates, issuing clipped instructions. Jack listened to the coded exchanges and felt the familiar tightening in his chest that came whenever a situation grew too large, too fast.

"Where are we taking Annie?" he asked.

"She's already en route to the same secure location," Chen said. "Full protection detail. She's as safe as we can make her."

Jack looked out the window as the vehicle pulled away from the hospital. He'd spent most of his career knowing that "safe" was a temporary condition. Determined people with resources and time could reach almost anyone. Sarah Mitchell had already proven that.

The safe house sat in a quiet suburban neighborhood, indistinguishable from the others on the street—neatly trimmed lawn, pale siding, a porch light just beginning to glow in the late afternoon. But Jack noticed the details immediately: the reinforced doorframe, the discreet exterior cameras, the way two agents casually occupied the neighboring driveway under the guise of talking beside a car.

Inside, the former living room had been converted into a temporary command center. Monitors glowed along one wall. Maps and building schematics were spread across folding tables. Radios crackled constantly, the low murmur of coordination filling the space.

Annie stood near the center of it, speaking quietly with one of the agents. She looked exhausted, strands of hair slipping loose from whatever quick tie she'd used, but her posture was steady, her attention focused. When she saw him, relief crossed her face before she masked it.

"How are you feeling?" she asked as they helped him into a chair.

"Like I made a series of questionable life choices involving gunfire and a mountainside," he said faintly. "But I'm here."

She exhaled, a sound that carried more emotion than she probably intended. "You're supposed to be in a hospital bed."

"And you're supposed to be running as far from this as possible," he replied. "Seems neither of us is good at following orders."

He accepted the medication one of the agents offered, grateful for the dulling edge it brought without fully clouding his mind. Then he looked past her to the map Agent Chen was spreading across the table.

"What's happening?" he asked.

Chen pointed to several marked locations. "We've identified possible sites for a controlled exchange."

"Exchange?" Jack repeated, and then he saw Annie's face.

Understanding hit.

"You're using the locket," he said slowly. "And you."

"I'm using the locket," Annie corrected, her voice calm. "I'm just the one who carries it."

"No." Jack pushed against the arms of the chair, pain flaring hot and bright. "Absolutely not. They've already tried to kill you. They burned your shop. They beat your uncle nearly to death. They turned a hospital into a hunting ground. You are not walking into another trap."

"Jack," she said, stepping closer, lowering her voice, "six people were injured today. People who had nothing to do with Eleanor. This doesn't stop unless we stop it."

He searched her face, hating that he recognized the resolve there. The same resolve that had once made her walk into cold case archives alone at midnight. The same resolve that had always put truth before comfort, justice before safety.

"Then I'm coming," he said.

Chen started to object, but Jack cut her off. "I won't be useful sitting in a chair listening to updates while Annie faces the person who's been orchestrating this. I know these people. I know how they think. And if anything goes wrong, you're not going to be able to stop me from acting, anyway."

Chen's jaw tightened as she looked between them, reading what neither of them said aloud.

"Fine," she said finally. "But you follow the operation plan. Exactly. No independent moves. No trying to protect each other at the expense of the mission."

"Agreed," Annie said.

Jack nodded.

As Chen began issuing orders and the room shifted into coordinated motion, Jack found his thoughts drifting—not to tactics, not to weapons or exits, but to a woman who had sat on a stone bench nearly a century ago, pregnant and afraid, and still chosen to hide the truth.

Eleanor Blackwood had known the cost.

She had paid it anyway.

And now the echo of that choice had reached them.

Jack closed his eyes briefly, anchoring himself to the weight of what they were about to do. Whatever waited on the other side of this operation, he knew one thing with clarity that cut through pain and fear alike.

They were done running.

And he would stand between Annie and whatever came next, whether it was justice—or the price Eleanor had paid to preserve it.

***

Jack gritted his teeth as the federal agents helped him transfer from the hospital bed to a wheelchair, every careful movement sending fresh waves of pain through his injured shoulder.

The wound throbbed with a deep, grinding heat that radiated down his arm and into his chest, a reminder that his body had not caught up with the urgency of the situation. The surgeon had been clear—he needed rest, immobility, time. What he was being prepared for now offered none of those things.

But there was no scenario in which he stayed behind while Annie Whitaker walked into danger alone.

"Detective, you don't have to do this," Agent Chen said as one of her agents adjusted the sling, supporting his arm. "We can handle the operation without you."

Jack forced himself to breathe through the pain before answering. "With respect, Agent Chen, you don't know these people the way I do. I've been inside their patterns for days now. I've watched how they move, how they escalate, how they calculate risk." He lifted his eyes to hers. "And I know Annie. I know exactly what she's willing to walk into if she believes it's the right thing to do."

Chen studied him for a moment, as if weighing the cost of arguing against the reality in his voice.

The evacuation route took them through service corridors and freight elevators, far from the public wings of the hospital. Even so, Jack caught fractured glimpses of the chaos they were leaving behind. Armed hospital security clustered at corridor intersections. Gurneys were being rushed through side halls.

A nurse stood pressed against a wall, one hand shaking as she spoke urgently into a phone. This was no longer a containment. It was a crisis.

"How many?" Jack asked quietly as they reached the parking garage.

"Six confirmed injured so far," Chen replied. "Three security guards, two nurses, one physician who was caught between floors."

Jack closed his eyes briefly. Six people whose only mistake had been showing up to work. Six lives pulled into violence because a family had spent a century protecting a lie.

They helped him into the back of an unmarked federal SUV, the seat cool and firm beneath him. Chen took the front passenger seat, already speaking into her radio, absorbing updates, issuing clipped instructions. Jack listened to the coded exchanges and felt the familiar tightening in his chest that came whenever a situation grew too large, too fast.

"Where are we taking Annie?" he asked.

"She's already en route to the same secure location," Chen said. "Full protection detail. She's as safe as we can make her."

Jack looked out the window as the vehicle pulled away from the hospital. He'd spent most of his career knowing that "safe" was a temporary condition. Determined people with resources and time could reach almost anyone. Sarah Mitchell had already proven that.

The safe house sat in a quiet suburban neighborhood, indistinguishable from the others on the street—neatly trimmed lawn, pale siding, a porch light just beginning to glow in the late afternoon. But Jack noticed the details immediately: the reinforced doorframe, the discreet exterior cameras, the way two agents casually occupied the neighboring driveway under the guise of talking beside a car.

Inside, the former living room had been converted into a temporary command center.

Monitors glowed along one wall. Maps and building schematics were spread across folding tables. Radios crackled constantly, the low murmur of coordination filling the space.

Annie stood near the center of it, speaking quietly with one of the agents. She looked exhausted, strands of hair slipping loose from whatever quick tie she'd used, but her posture was steady, her attention focused. When she saw him, relief crossed her face before she masked it.

"How are you feeling?" she asked as they helped him into a chair.

"Like I made a series of questionable life choices involving gunfire and a mountainside," he said faintly. "But I'm here."

She exhaled, a sound that carried more emotion than she probably intended. "You're supposed to be in a hospital bed."

"And you're supposed to be running as far from this as possible," he replied. "Seems neither of us is good at following orders."

He accepted the medication one of the agents offered, grateful for the dulling edge it brought without fully clouding his mind. Then he looked past her to the map Agent Chen was spreading across the table.

"What's happening?" he asked.

Chen pointed to several marked locations. "We've identified possible sites for a controlled exchange."

"Exchange?" Jack repeated, and then he saw Annie's face.

Understanding hit.

"You're using the locket," he said slowly. "And you."

"I'm using the locket," Annie corrected, her voice calm. "I'm just the one who carries it."

"No." Jack pushed against the arms of the chair, pain flaring hot and bright. "Absolutely not. They've already tried to kill you. They burned your shop. They beat your uncle nearly to death. They turned a hospital into a hunting ground. You are not walking into another trap."

"Jack," she said, stepping closer, lowering her voice, "six people were injured today. People who had nothing to do with Eleanor. This doesn't stop unless we stop it."

He searched her face, hating that he recognized the resolve there. The same resolve that had once made her walk into cold case archives alone at midnight. The same resolve that had always put truth before comfort, justice before safety.

"Then I'm coming," he said.

Chen started to object, but Jack cut her off. "I won't be useful sitting in a chair listening to updates while Annie faces the person who's been orchestrating this. I know these people. I know how they think. And if anything goes wrong, you're not going to be able to stop me from acting, anyway."

Chen's jaw tightened as she looked between them, reading what neither of them said aloud.

"Fine," she said finally. "But you follow the operation plan. Exactly. No independent moves. No trying to protect each other at the expense of the mission."

"Agreed," Annie said.

Jack nodded.

As Chen began issuing orders and the room shifted into coordinated motion, Jack found his thoughts drifting—not to tactics, not to weapons or exits, but to a woman who had sat on a stone bench nearly a century ago, pregnant and afraid, and still chosen to hide the truth.

Eleanor Blackwood had known the cost.

She had paid for it anyway.

And now the echo of that choice had reached them.

Jack closed his eyes briefly, anchoring himself to the weight of what they were about to do. Whatever waited on the other side of this operation, he knew one thing with clarity that cut through pain and fear alike.

They were done running.

And he would stand between Annie and whatever came next, whether it was justice—or the price Eleanor had paid to preserve it.

Chapter 15

The First National Bank of Fairview looked deceptively ordinary in the afternoon sunlight, its brick façade and traditional columns giving no hint of the secrets sealed inside its vault.

Annie sat in the back seat of the unmarked federal vehicle, watching people pass on the sidewalk with paper bags and coffee cups, unaware that less than a hundred feet away, a century of lies was about to be opened.

Federal agents moved in controlled patterns around the building, radios murmuring softly, their presence understated but unmistakable. It felt surreal that something so carefully orchestrated could unfold in a place where people came to deposit checks and ask about mortgages.

"Remember," Agent Chen said quietly as they prepared to exit the vehicle, "we don't know what we're going to find in that box. It may be exactly what Eleanor described, or it may raise new questions. Either way, everything is documented, every item logged, and we treat whatever we uncover as potentially critical to dismantling Sarah Mitchell's organization."

Annie nodded, her fingers pressing unconsciously against the locket in her pocket. Eleanor's key rested warm against her skin, as though it had been waiting all these years for this moment. "What about Sarah Mitchell?" she asked. "Have you located her?"

"We're tracking several possibilities," Chen replied as they stepped onto the sidewalk. "She's careful. People like her build layers between themselves and exposure. That's why today matters. If Eleanor preserved what we think she did, it gives us leverage. She can't outrun."

Inside, the bank smelled faintly of polished wood and paper. Mr. Henderson, the bank manager, met them near the entrance with a nervous efficiency that betrayed how far outside his normal responsibilities this day had already gone. He led them through the public floor, past the teller stations and closed offices, and into a secured elevator that descended toward the vault.

"Box 247 has been in our records since 1927," he explained as the doors slid shut. "It was rented by Eleanor Blackwood. According to our files, the fees were paid in advance for ninety-nine years."

"Ninety-nine," Annie repeated softly. The number settled into her chest. Eleanor hadn't planned for discovery. She had planned for endurance.

The vault level was cool and hushed, rows of metal boxes stretching into precise infinity. Mr. Henderson stopped before a small door etched with the number 247. "We'll need both keys and federal authorization."

Annie removed the tiny brass key from the locket. The metal trembled faintly between her fingers as she handed it over. Mr. Henderson inserted it. Agent Chen turned the master key. The lock disengaged with a muted click that echoed far louder in Annie's mind than it should have.

After ninety-six years, Eleanor Blackwood's voice was about to be heard.

The box was placed on a table. Mr. Henderson stepped away. Chen nodded to Annie.

She lifted the lid.

Photographs lay on top—neatly stacked, carefully protected. Annie picked one up, her breath catching as she recognized Richard

Mitchell, younger but unmistakable, posed in the shadowed interior of what could only be an illegal Prohibition-era club.

Other photos followed. Richard with known bootleggers. Richard with men later arrested for violent crimes. Richard standing beside crates marked with shipping codes Annie recognized from historical law enforcement records.

But it was what lay beneath the photographs that shifted the air in the room.

Ledgers.

Thick, leather-bound books filled edge to edge with Eleanor's handwriting.

"She recorded everything," Annie murmured as she opened one, scanning columns of figures, names, and coded notes. "Transactions. Transfers. Payments to officials." Her eyes lifted slowly to Agent Chen. "This isn't just family theft. This is the foundation of a criminal network."

The pages documented bootlegging operations, shell companies, laundered profits, bribes, and early connections to syndicates in Chicago and New York. Richard Mitchell hadn't simply stolen a business. He had built an empire in fraud and blood.

"Eleanor wasn't just preserving proof of her own murder," Annie said quietly. "She was documenting the birth of something that never stopped."

At the bottom of the box, wrapped in carefully sealed oilcloth, lay two final documents.

Annie unfolded the first and felt her pulse stutter.

A birth certificate.

Thomas Blackwood Jr.

Born March 12, 1927.

"She had her son," Annie whispered.

Then she unfolded the second.

Death certificate.

Thomas Blackwood Jr.

Age: five days.

Cause of death: injuries sustained during violent assault.

The room seemed to tilt.

"Someone killed him," Agent Chen said, her voice low and precise. "This wasn't illness. This was murder."

Annie pressed her hand to the edge of the table as nausea rose. Richard Mitchell hadn't just murdered Eleanor. He had eliminated the heir who could have stripped him of everything.

"But the estate," Annie said slowly. "If her son died, the inheritance should have passed to her daughters."

Chen was already photographing the documents. "Mary and Joy."

Annie's breath came shallow. "Joy was my grandmother."

Which meant Uncle Eric.

At the very bottom of the box lay a final page, preserved as carefully as the rest. Eleanor's handwriting flowed across it in controlled, elegant lines. A will.

In it, Eleanor left all claims to her daughters and their descendants. She named Richard Mitchell's inheritance fraudulent. She recorded his crimes. She placed her faith not in law, but in time.

Annie stared at the paper, understanding settling like weight into her bones.

Uncle Eric had not just been attacked for answers.

He had been targeted because he stood at the end of a bloodline Richard Mitchell had tried to erase.

And Eleanor had ensured that even death would not finish the work he began.

***

Jack paced the length of the safe house living room despite the steady burn in his shoulder, his frustration tightening with every turn. Annie and Agent Chen had been at the bank for over two hours, and the absence of updates pressed against him harder than the pain ever could.

He understood the operational reasons for keeping him back, understood the logic behind command centers and controlled distances, but logic didn't quiet the instinct that told him he was in the wrong place. Annie was facing the heart of this case, and he was sitting in a borrowed house with federal equipment humming where a dining table should have been.

"Any word?" he asked, stopping near the bank of radios Agent Martinez monitored.

"They're still inside the vault level," Martinez replied, eyes flicking between screens and instruments. "So far, everything is proceeding according to plan. Detective, you really should sit down. That shoulder isn't doing you any favors."

Jack gave a short shake of his head and resumed pacing. He could still smell the mountain rain in his clothes, still hear Annie's breathing in his ear from that final walk to the highway. Sitting still felt like surrender, and he had done enough of that four years ago.

His phone vibrated.

He reached for it instantly, expecting Agent Chen's name. Instead, an unfamiliar number glowed on the screen, followed by words that iced his spine.

Your girlfriend is at First National Bank. Interesting choice. Did you know my great-grandfather helped found that board? History has long roots in Fairview. So do loyalties.

Jack's hand tightened around the phone.

"Martinez," he said sharply. "Get Chen on the line. Now."

Martinez was already reaching for the radio. Jack stepped closer and held out the screen. The agent read it once, then again, his jaw tightening.

"If the Mitchell family helped establish that bank," Martinez said slowly, "they could have legacy access. Old accounts. Institutional blind spots. Maybe even people on staff who still owe them favors."

"They may have been watching that box for decades," Jack said. "Waiting."

Before Martinez could respond, the radios exploded into layered voices and clipped codes.

"All units, be advised—we have an active shooter situation at First National Bank. Multiple armed individuals have breached the building. Repeat, active shooter at First National Bank."

The room seemed to tilt.

Jack's mind leaped instantly to Annie underground in the vault corridors, to narrow passages and limited exits, to her standing over Eleanor's box when violence found her again.

"I'm going," he said, already turning toward the door.

Martinez caught his arm. "Detective, you are not cleared—"

"Get your people moving," Jack cut in. "Coordinate with local law enforcement. Do whatever the book tells you to do. But I'm not staying here."

"You're wounded," Martinez insisted. "And walking into an unknown, hostile situation without tactical support."

"I'm walking into a place where Annie Whitaker is in immediate danger," Jack said, his voice low and immovable. "That's the only calculation that matters."

His phone vibrated again.

> Come alone, Detective. No agents. No teams. No heroics. Just you. And maybe this ends without more blood.

Jack stared at the screen, recognizing the construction of the message as clearly as any crime scene. Isolation. Control. A funnel into their chosen ground.

A trap.

Also, an opening.

"Martinez," he said, checking the magazine in his weapon and gathering what he could manage one-handed. "Tell Chen what just came through. Tell her Sarah Mitchell is inside the bank, and she wants me there. Personally."

"This is suicide," Martinez said.

"No," Jack replied quietly. "This is what Eleanor Blackwood never got. Someone walking toward the threat instead of away from it."

Outside, he slid into his vehicle, the engine's vibration traveling straight through his injured shoulder, but he welcomed the pain. It kept him anchored. Focused.

The drive took twelve minutes. Twelve minutes of sirens bleeding into the air from every direction. Twelve minutes of rehearsing corridors, vault levels, stairwells, hostage response scenarios. Twelve minutes of thinking about Eleanor hiding truth in darkness, about Annie refusing to run from it, about how close he had come to losing her to fear before danger ever touched them.

By the time he reached the bank, emergency vehicles crowded the street. Law enforcement had established a perimeter, but the building itself had gone blind. Its windows were blacked out from within, sealing whatever was happening behind brick and glass.

His phone rang.

He answered.

"Detective Calloway," Sarah Mitchell said, her voice smooth, controlled, almost polite. "You can see we're holding your people in a rather inconvenient position."

"What do you want, Sarah?"

"A trade," she said. "You come inside. Alone. Unarmed. And I release Agent Chen, Annie Whitaker, and the employees who had the misfortune of being present today."

"And if I don't."

"Then we begin removing lives from the equation." Her voice cooled. "You have ten minutes."

The call ended.

Jack lowered the phone slowly and looked at the bank's sealed front doors, at the hidden war behind them, at the woman he loved somewhere inside.

The choice wasn't impossible—it was inevitable. Some truths demanded witnesses, others demanded defenders, and some demanded someone willing to step into the dark and hold the line. Jack moved toward the entrance.

Chapter 16

ANNIE PRESSED HERSELF AGAINST the cold marble wall of the bank vault, her heart hammering as chaos erupted somewhere above them. Gunfire had broken out only minutes after they finished documenting Eleanor's evidence, sharp cracks echoing through the floors overhead, followed by shouting voices and the shrill wail of security alarms.

"Stay down," Agent Chen whispered, her weapon drawn as she positioned herself near the vault entrance. "My team upstairs isn't responding to radio calls."

The bank manager, Mr. Henderson, huddled behind one of the larger safe deposit units, his face drained of color. "There's only one way out of this vault," he said, his voice shaking. "The elevator we came down in. If they control that—"

"Then we're trapped," Annie finished quietly.

She tightened her grip on the leather portfolio holding Eleanor's documents. Inside it lay proof of murder, proof of inheritance fraud, proof that the Mitchell empire had been built on stolen blood. The birth certificate alone could dismantle nearly a century of lies. Sarah Mitchell wouldn't hesitate to kill for it. She already had.

Agent Chen lowered her radio, frustration tightening her expression. "We're getting some chatter. Multiple armed hostiles in the building—at least six. They've secured the main banking floor and are demanding access to the vault level."

"How long before they reach us?" Annie asked.

"That depends on whether they override the security system or force their way through," Chen replied, checking her ammunition. "Either way, we need to assume ten to fifteen minutes."

Annie scanned the vault, forcing herself to think instead of panic. Thick walls. Limited access points. Heavy doors. A stronghold—if you were defending. A coffin if you were trapped.

"Mr. Henderson," she said suddenly, "is there any other way out? Service corridors, maintenance tunnels, anything at all?"

He hesitated, then nodded slowly. "There is a maintenance passage. It connects to the building's utility system and runs under the parking garage next door. It's barely wide enough for one person, and I don't even know if it's still usable."

"Show us," Agent Chen said.

They moved quickly through the vault's far end into a narrow corridor lined with aging electrical panels and humming machinery. Almost hidden behind one large box was a small metal door marked

AUTHORIZED PERSONNEL ONLY.

"This is it," Henderson said, pulling out a ring of keys. "Installed in the sixties. It hasn't been used in years."

Chen tested the door and peered into the narrow darkness beyond. "It's tight, but it's a way out. Where does it come up?"

"Basement level of the parking garage. Near the utility room. From there, you can reach the street without going back through the bank."

It wasn't much, but it was movement. And movement meant survival.

"We go," Chen said. "Together. And we assume they may know about this route."

As they prepared to enter the passage, Annie's phone vibrated in her hand.

Jack.

"Answer it," Chen said quietly.

"Jack?" Annie pressed the phone to her ear, relief crashing through her so hard it almost hurt.

"Annie, thank God. Are you hurt? Are you safe?"

"We're in the vault. They've taken the building, but we found another way out." She spoke quickly, explaining about the tunnel as Chen signaled for Henderson to open the door.

Jack didn't respond right away. When he did, his voice had changed. "Sarah called me. She wants a trade. Me for you and the hostages. She gave me ten minutes."

Annie's blood went cold. "No. Jack, no. That's exactly what she wants. It's a trap."

"Of course it is. But if I don't go, she's going to start killing people—employees, customers, agents. Innocent people."

"And if you do go, she'll kill you," Annie said, fighting to keep her voice steady. "We have the evidence. We can expose her. We can end this without you sacrificing yourself."

"What good is the truth if people die while we're protecting it?" he asked quietly. "I've already decided. I'm going in."

"Then I'm coming with you."

"No." His voice hardened. "You're getting out. You're taking Eleanor's evidence somewhere safe. You're making sure this case is finished. That's how we honor her—by making sure the truth survives."

Behind her, metal groaned at the vault entrance. Someone was working on the systems.

"Jack, I love you," Annie said, the words breaking free before fear could stop them. "I'm not losing you. Not again."

His breath caught. "If something happens to me, remember that these past days with you were the best of my life. Remember that I finally stopped being afraid—and that it was because of you."

The call ended.

Annie stared at the screen, her hands shaking, tears blurring the numbers. Jack was walking into Sarah Mitchell's trap, and every instinct in her screamed to run toward him instead of away.

"Ms. Whitaker," Agent Chen said gently. "We have to move."

Annie wiped her face and drew in a breath that burned. Jack was buying them time. She wouldn't waste it—but she wouldn't abandon him either.

"Agent Chen," she said as they turned toward the tunnel, "how long until your teams are fully in position around the bank?"

Chen studied her. "They're close. Why?"

"Because I have an idea," Annie said quietly. "And it might be the only way to stop this without letting Jack walk into that building alone."

***

Jack sat in his car in the bank parking lot, surrounded by police vehicles and emergency responders, knowing that he was about to walk into what would probably be the last ten minutes of his life.

His shoulder throbbed with each heartbeat, and the pain medication was wearing off, but his mind was crystal clear.

This is how it ends, he thought. Not in Some dramatic firefight or heroic last stand, but in a trade. My life for the lives of innocent people who got caught up in a century-old conspiracy.

It wasn't the ending he would have chosen, but it was the ending that felt right. Eleanor Blackwood had sacrificed her life to preserve the truth. Now it was his turn to make a similar choice.

His phone rang one final time, and Jack answered it knowing who would be on the other end.

"Detective Calloway." Sarah Mitchell's voice was crisp, professional, almost businesslike. "I trust you've made your decision."

"I'll come in," Jack said simply. "But I want to see proof that the hostages are alive and unharmed before I surrender my weapon."

"Of course. We're not monsters, Detective. We're simply businesspeople protecting our family's legitimate interests."

Legitimate interests. The phrase would have been laughable if the situation weren't so deadly serious. Sarah Mitchell had convinced herself that murder, arson, and hostage-taking were justified because they protected her claim to a fortune built on inheritance fraud.

"I'm walking to the front entrance now," Jack said, getting out of his car despite the shouted protests from the police officers who'd been trying to keep him away from the bank. "I'm armed, but I'll surrender my weapon at the door."

"Excellent. And Detective? Please don't do anything heroic. We both know how those gestures typically end."

Jack hung up and began walking across the parking lot toward the bank's main entrance. Every step felt surreal, like he was watching Someone else make the decision to trade his life for the lives of strangers. But as he approached the building where Annie was trapped, he realized that this didn't feel like sacrifice at all.

It felt like coming home.

The bank's front doors opened as he approached, and Jack found himself face to face with two men in tactical gear carrying assault rifles. Professional mercenaries, just as he'd expected.

"Weapon," one of them said curtly.

Jack slowly drew his service pistol and placed it on the ground, then stepped back with his hands visible. One of the mercenaries kicked the gun away while the other kept his rifle trained on Jack's chest.

"Inside," the first mercenary ordered.

The bank's main floor had been transformed into a command center, with electronic equipment set up on customer service desks and additional armed men positioned at strategic points around the room. Bank employees and customers sat on the floor near the teller windows, their faces reflecting the terror of people caught in the wrong place at the wrong time.

But it was the woman standing near the bank manager's office who commanded Jack's attention. Sarah Mitchell was smaller than he'd expected, well-dressed and professional-looking, with the kind of quiet confidence that came from wealth and power. She looked like Someone who belonged in a boardroom, not Someone orchestrating a hostage situation.

"Detective Calloway," she said, approaching him with a slight smile. "Thank you for being so reasonable. Your cooperation will save several lives today."

"Where are Agent Chen and Annie Whitaker?" Jack demanded.

"Safe, for the moment. They're in the vault level with Some of my associates, examining what I'm told are Some very interesting historical documents." Sarah's smile sharpened. "Documents that belong to my family, by the way. Documents that were stolen from us nearly a century ago by a disturbed woman who couldn't accept that her husband's business dealings were perfectly legal."

Jack almost laughed at the audacity of the lie. "You really believe that, don't you? You really think Eleanor Blackwood was the criminal in this situation."

"I think Eleanor Blackwood was an unstable woman who fabricated evidence to cover her own tracks when she abandoned her family," Sarah replied coolly. "And I think you and Ms. Whitaker have been duped by a very sophisticated hoax."

"Then why are you so desperate to get the evidence back? If it's fake, why not let it become public and expose the hoax?"

For the first time, Sarah's composure cracked slightly. "Because even fake evidence can be damaging when it's presented convincingly. Because there are people who would use fabricated documents to make frivolous legal claims against my family's assets. Because Sometimes, Detective, the truth matters less than public perception."

Jack studied her face, looking for any sign of genuine belief in what she was saying. But what he saw instead was the calculating expression of Someone who knew exactly what crimes her family had committed and was willing to do anything to protect the fortune those crimes had built.

"You know Eleanor was telling the truth," he said quietly. "You know your great-grandfather murdered her and her infant son. You know your family's entire fortune is built on inheritance fraud. And you know that eventually, the truth is going to come out."

"The truth, Detective, is whatever people choose to believe. And dead people don't testify in court."

The threat was unmistakable, and Jack felt a chill of fear that had nothing to do with his own safety. Sarah Mitchell wasn't just planning to kill him—she was planning to eliminate everyone who'd seen Eleanor's evidence.

But as he looked around the bank at the electronic equipment and the coordinated positioning of her mercenaries, Jack realized that Something about the situation didn't feel right. It was too organized, too professional, too elaborate for what should have been a simple evidence-retrieval operation.

Unless retrieving the evidence isn't the real goal, he thought. Unless this whole hostage situation is a distraction from Something else.

"Sarah," he said, using her first name deliberately. "What's your exit strategy? You've got federal agents, local police, probably SWAT teams surrounding this building. How exactly do you plan to get out of here alive?"

Her smile was cold and confident. "Who says we're planning to get out, Detective? Sometimes the most effective way to end a problem is to make sure there's no evidence left to examine."

Jack's blood turned to ice as he understood her implication. Sarah Mitchell wasn't planning to escape with Eleanor's evidence.

She was planning to destroy the entire bank, along with everyone inside it.

Chapter 17

ANNIE CRAWLED THROUGH THE maintenance tunnel on her hands and knees, the narrow metal passage scraping her back and shoulders with every inch she moved forward. The air was stale and carried the faint tang of rust and old oil, and the darkness was so complete she could not see her own hands in front of her face.

Behind her, Agent Chen and Mr. Henderson followed in single file, their breathing loud in the confined space, every sound magnified by the hollow walls.

The leather portfolio containing Eleanor's evidence was secured against Annie's back with a strap taken from Henderson's tool kit, its weight steady and insistent, like a physical reminder of the truth she carried and the lives already lost to protect it.

"Not much farther," Henderson whispered from somewhere behind her. "The tunnel curves around the foundation and opens into the parking garage utility room. Fifty yards. Maybe less."

Annie nodded, even though he couldn't see her. Each movement sent a dull ache through her wrists and knees, and she had to force herself not to think about the mountain of concrete and steel above them. The tunnel had not been built for comfort. It had been built to hide pipes, wiring, and emergency systems no one wanted to see.

She focused instead on the slow rhythm of her breathing and the scrape of fabric against metal, counting each movement as proof that she was still moving forward.

Jack is walking into that building right now, she thought. He's stepping straight into her hands so we can get out.

The knowledge tightened her chest and drove her on. Jack hadn't hesitated. He hadn't bargained. He had made the decision the way Eleanor must have once made hers—with a terrible calm that came from knowing the cost and accepting it anyway.

"Wait," Agent Chen murmured suddenly.

Annie froze, heart hammering, as Chen shifted behind her and brought her radio closer. A wash of static filled the narrow space, punctuated by broken fragments of urgent voices.

"—signal interference—can't get clean telemetry—"

"—thermal anomalies in the basement—multiple concentrated heat points—"

"—possible jamming equipment in operation—"

Annie's breath caught. A cold, unwelcome clarity began assembling itself in her mind, piece by piece, as the words threaded together.

"Agent Chen," she whispered. "What if she's not here to recover the evidence at all?"

Chen's voice was low, controlled. "Explain."

"What if this whole thing is a diversion?" Annie said. "What if the hostage situation isn't the endgame? What if Sarah Mitchell doesn't want the evidence back—what if she wants to destroy it? And everyone who's seen it?"

Silence followed, heavy and immediate.

"That would explain the interference," Chen said slowly. "Large-scale jamming equipment. Signal disruption. Thermal readings that don't match human movement alone."

"And it would explain why Jack said it felt wrong," Annie pressed. "Why this operation is so big? So coordinated. She's not planning to leave with anything. She's planning to erase it."

The truth of it settled like ice in Annie's veins. If Sarah Mitchell had placed explosives throughout the building, then Jack hadn't walked into a negotiation. He had walked into a tomb.

"She's going to bring the whole place down," Annie whispered. "The evidence. The hostages. Her own people. Everyone."

Chen exhaled slowly. "If that's true, then this is no longer a hostage incident. This is a mass-casualty event."

The words sharpened Annie's fear into something focused and fierce. She began crawling again, faster now, ignoring the sting in her knees and the burn in her shoulders as the tunnel sloped upward.

"There," Henderson said urgently. "I see light."

A faint gray glow appeared ahead, growing brighter with each movement. Annie surged forward, dragging herself the last few feet until the tunnel opened abruptly into a cramped utility room beneath the parking garage. She rolled onto her side and pushed herself upright, muscles shaking from the effort.

The space smelled of cleaning chemicals and dust, and exposed pipes ran along the ceiling. A single fluorescent bulb buzzed overhead.

Agent Chen emerged moments later, already speaking into her radio, her voice clipped and commanding as she relayed what they had heard.

"Confirm thermal signatures again. I want precise readings. Are we looking at mechanical heat or chemical sources?"

Static answered, followed by a strained reply. "Ma'am, we're confident it's explosive material. Multiple devices. Placement suggests structural targeting."

Annie closed her eyes briefly. Structural targeting meant collapse. It meant Sarah Mitchell wasn't planning an escape. She was planning annihilation.

"Time estimate?" Chen asked.

"We don't have one. Jamming is preventing remote diagnostics."

Annie swallowed. No countdown. No visible clock. Just a building filled with people and the possibility that any second might be the last.

Chen turned sharply toward the door leading up into the garage. "We evacuate the surrounding blocks immediately. If she's set enough charges to compromise the foundation—"

"No." Annie's voice cut through the space, stronger than she felt. "We can't just pull back and wait."

Chen met her gaze. "Ms. Whitaker, if that building detonates—"

"Jack is in there," Annie said. "And so are bank employees, customers, and your agents. And if that evidence is destroyed, if Eleanor's records vanish, then she dies all over again. Everything she endured means nothing."

Chen's expression tightened, torn between protocol and the reality in Annie's eyes.

"Get the evidence out," Annie continued, gripping the straps of the portfolio. "Get it to a secure federal facility. To prosecutors. To someone who can make sure the truth is preserved. But I'm not leaving Jack inside that building."

"Annie, going back in—"

"I'm not going back through the front," Annie said. Her mind was already racing ahead, searching old maps, remembered conversations, anything she'd ever absorbed about Fairview's buildings and buried history. "But there may be another way."

She pulled out her phone, hands steadier than she expected, and dialed.

"Fairview Fire Department, this is Carmen."

"Carmen, this is Annie Whitaker. From the apartment fire."

"Annie? Are you okay?"

"I'm safe. But there's an active hostage and explosives situation at First National Bank. I need to know if there are any underground connections to that building."

There was a pause, and Annie imagined Carmen's brow furrowing the way it had when she studied blueprints.

"The bank connects to the old courthouse," Carmen said slowly. "There's a sub-basement service tunnel. Built in the forties. Emergency evacuation route. It's not on most public schematics."

Annie's pulse leaped. "Where does it enter the courthouse?"

"Basement level. Behind records storage. It's sealed, but the access door should still be there."

"Can you meet me there?" Annie asked. "Now."

Another pause. "Annie...if there are explosives—"

"Then people don't have much time," Annie said gently. "And Jack Calloway is in that building."

"I'll be there in five minutes," Carmen said. "I'm calling in backup."

Annie ended the call and turned back to Agent Chen. "The courthouse connects underground. There's a tunnel to the bank's substructure. If anyone can navigate a compromised structure and move people out, it's the fire department."

Chen considered that for a brief, charged moment. Then she nodded sharply. "All right. We'll move. But the evidence goes now."

Two agents stepped forward. Annie hesitated, fingers tightening around the straps, then forced herself to release them. "Promise me it won't disappear," she said quietly.

"It won't," Chen said. "And neither will you."

They split at the garage entrance. Federal vehicles pulled away with the portfolio secured inside, while Annie and Chen headed on foot toward the courthouse, sirens and shouting echoing through the surrounding streets. Fairview no longer looked like her hometown. It looked like a city under siege.

As they ran, Annie's thoughts returned to Eleanor—not as a victim, but as a woman who had stood at the edge of her own ending and chosen to act anyway. Eleanor had hidden the truth believing someone, someday, would be brave enough to retrieve it.

"Help me be brave enough," Annie whispered.

The courthouse rose ahead of them, its old stone face calm and indifferent. Carmen's engine was already pulling up, lights flashing. She jumped out before it fully stopped.

"Show me," Annie said.

Carmen led them through a side entrance and down a narrow staircase into the basement. The air grew cooler, the walls thicker. Rows of shelving gave way to older brick and sealed doors. Carmen stopped in front of one, dust heavy on its surface.

"This is it."

Together, they wrenched it open.

Darkness waited beyond.

Annie stepped forward, heart pounding, knowing with a terrible certainty that Jack was somewhere beneath her feet, standing inside a building wired to die.

And she was not going to leave him there.

***

Jack stood in the bank's main lobby, watching Sarah Mitchell's mercenaries position themselves around the room with military precision. The hostages—bank employees and customers who'd been in the wrong place at the wrong time—sat on the floor near the teller windows, their faces reflecting a mixture of terror and desperate hope.

But it was the electronic equipment that commanded Jack's attention. Laptops, communication devices, and what looked like remote detonation controls were set up on multiple desks throughout the room. This wasn't just a hostage situation—it was a command center for Something much larger and more destructive.

"Admiring our setup?" Sarah Mitchell asked, approaching him with that same cold smile. "We've spent considerable time and resources planning this operation."

"Planning to blow up a building full of innocent people?" Jack kept his voice steady despite the fury building in his chest. "That's what this is about, isn't it? You're not just trying to steal Eleanor's evidence—you're planning to destroy it completely, along with everyone who's seen it."

"I'm planning to end a problem that's been threatening my family for nearly a century," Sarah replied coolly. "Eleanor Blackwood created a fiction, a elaborate hoax designed to cover her own crimes.

That fiction has now attracted the attention of federal investigators and misguided amateur detectives who think they can rewrite history."

"So you're going to rewrite it with explosives?"

"I'm going to erase it completely. When this building comes down, there will be no evidence left to examine, no witnesses left to testify, no loose ends for future investigators to pursue." Sarah gestured toward the electronic equipment. "Sometimes, Detective, the most elegant solution is also the most final one."

Jack studied the setup more carefully, noting the positioning of the detonation controls and the way Sarah's men were maintaining distance from certain areas of the building. "How long do we have?"

"That depends on you, Detective. My associates downstairs are currently retrieving the documents that Ms. Whitaker found in the safe deposit box. Once they've confirmed that we have all of Eleanor's so-called evidence, we'll evacuate our people and trigger the charges."

"And the hostages?"

"Will unfortunately be caught in what appears to be a tragic gas explosion. These old buildings, you know—so many potential hazards with the aging infrastructure."

Jack felt sick as he realized the scope of Sarah's plan. She was going to make the explosion look like an accident, eliminating all evidence of the Mitchell family's crimes while simultaneously getting rid of everyone who could testify about what they'd discovered.

"There's one problem with your plan," Jack said. "Agent Chen's backup teams know exactly what you're doing. They've detected your jamming equipment and identified the explosive devices. Even if you succeed in destroying this building, the federal investigation will continue."

"Will it?" Sarah's smile was genuinely amused. "Detective, do you really think we haven't planned for that contingency? Do you think this operation exists in isolation?"

Before Jack could ask what she meant, his attention was drawn to movement near the bank's rear entrance. Through the glass doors, he could see figures in tactical gear moving through what appeared to be a service corridor.

Annie. The thought hit him like a physical blow. Despite his instructions to escape through the maintenance tunnel, despite the obvious danger, she was coming back for him.

"Ah," Sarah said, following his gaze. "It appears Ms. Whitaker is more resourceful than we anticipated. How romantic—she's come back to die with you."

Jack felt a surge of fear and anger unlike anything he'd ever experienced. "Sarah, if you hurt her—"

"You'll what, Detective? You're unarmed, outnumbered, and surrounded by enough explosives to level this entire city block. What exactly do you think you can do to me?"

But even as she spoke, Jack was calculating distances, positions, possibilities. The detonation controls were about twenty feet away, guarded by two mercenaries. The hostages were positioned between him and the rear entrance where Annie would be entering. And Sarah Mitchell was standing close enough that he might be able to reach her before her men could stop him.

It wasn't much of a plan, but it was all he had.

"You're right," Jack said, taking a small step closer to Sarah. "I can't stop you. But I can make sure you don't get to enjoy your victory."

"What are you—"

Jack lunged forward, tackling Sarah Mitchell to the floor just as the rear entrance exploded inward in a shower of glass and smoke. Federal agents poured through the opening, their weapons ready, their voices shouting commands that were barely audible over the chaos.

But as Jack struggled with Sarah on the marble floor, he caught sight of the detonation controls on the nearby desk. One of the screens was flashing red, and numbers were counting down rapidly.

00:47... 00:46... 00:45...

Sarah had triggered the explosives. The building was going to come down in less than a minute, and there was no way to evacuate all the hostages in time.

Unless Someone could reach the detonation controls and stop the countdown.

Jack looked across the chaotic lobby and saw Annie fighting her way through the firefight toward the electronic equipment. She'd seen the countdown too, and she was trying to reach the controls before time ran out.

Please God, Jack prayed as gunfire erupted around them and the countdown continued its relentless march toward zero. Let her be fast enough. Let her be brave enough. Let her save all of us.

But as he watched Annie dodge between armed mercenaries and desperate hostages, Jack realized that their survival depended on more than just courage and speed.

It depended on Eleanor Blackwood's legacy of never giving up, even in the face of certain death.

Chapter 18

ANNIE DOVE BEHIND AN overturned desk as gunfire chewed into the marble wall above her, stone dust stinging her face while her heart battered against her ribs.

The world narrowed to noise and motion and the furious red pulse of the countdown display across the lobby, its numbers burning into her vision as if they had branded themselves there. Thirty-eight seconds. That was all the time she had to reach the detonation controls and stop explosives designed to tear the building—and everyone inside it—apart.

She pressed her forehead briefly to the cool floor and forced herself to breathe, forcing air into lungs that wanted to seize. Think. Not like a victim. Not like a hostage. Think like Eleanor. Eleanor had faced this same certainty of death and still found a way to outmaneuver it.

She had been watched. Trapped. Silenced. And yet she had preserved the truth so carefully that it had survived nearly a century of lies. Eleanor had not panicked. She had planned. She had hidden. She had believed that even if she fell, someone else would rise and carry the truth forward.

If Eleanor Blackwood could outwit a killer with nothing but ink, paper, and faith, Annie could out think a machine.

"Annie!"

Jack's voice cut through the chaos, rough with strain and urgency. She saw him across the lobby, still locked with Sarah Mitchell on the marble floor, federal agents moving in disciplined arcs around them as mercenaries were forced back or taken down. "The red button! Try the red button!"

Annie lifted her head and risked a glance toward the command setup. Screens glowed across several desks, cables feeding into a central control unit dense with switches and digital readouts. It looked overwhelming—too many systems, too many possibilities, too little time.

But there, unmistakable even in the chaos, was a large red button clearly marked in block letters: EMERGENCY STOP.

Sometimes criminals overcomplicated things. Sometimes they still built in the same fail-safes everyone else did. Annie broke from cover and sprinted, weaving between fallen chairs and shattered glass as federal gunfire cracked behind her.

She felt the displacement of bullets more than she heard them, thin invisible lines of danger snapping past her skin. Twenty-eight seconds. Her shoes skidded as she hit the polished floor near the desk. She grabbed the edge, hauled herself upright, and reached for the controls—

—and froze.

Another timer glowed on a secondary monitor. Independent. Active. Unstopped. Twelve seconds. Cold poured through her veins. This was never meant to be disabled easily. Sarah hadn't built one system. She'd built layers. Redundancies. Insurance. Sarah had planned for someone like her.

"Jack!" Annie shouted, her voice tearing loose from her chest. "There's a backup timer! Twelve seconds!"

Across the lobby she saw his face change—not fear, not even shock, but something dangerously close to acceptance, as if he were already bracing himself for the ending. No. Not like this. Not when

Eleanor's voice had finally been heard. Not when they had fought this hard to bring truth into the light.

Annie slammed her palm onto the emergency stop. The main display froze at sixteen seconds. But the secondary counter kept going. Eight seconds. The lobby had begun to shift as agents shouted evacuation orders, pulling hostages to their feet, dragging the wounded toward exits. Annie knew what they all knew. There was no time.

Her gaze flew over the backup panel. Fewer controls. Simpler interface. One guarded switch stood out from the rest.

MANUAL OVERRIDE.

She had no idea what it actually did. No schematic. No training. No margin for error. Her hand hovered inches above the switch, her mind screaming with every possible outcome. Manual overrides could disable. They could reset. They could trigger.

She thought of Eleanor, hand pressed to her stomach, whispering promises she didn't know how to keep. She thought of ink pressed hard into paper because silence was no longer an option.

She thought of Jack running into darkness because he loved her too much to let anyone else pay the price.

Eleanor hadn't known the outcome either.

She had only known what was right.

Annie flipped the switch.

The backup timer stopped at 00:01.

For a heartbeat, the lobby didn't breathe. Then sound rushed back in—shouting, sobbing, commands, radios crackling as if the building itself had exhaled. Annie stayed frozen, staring at the halted display, her brain refusing to accept that the world hadn't ended.

"We need EOD in here now," Agent Chen was already saying into her radio. "Multiple devices. Countdown interrupted, not disarmed."

Annie's legs finally gave way. She sank against the desk, fingers still braced against the equipment as if it might suddenly change its mind. They were alive. The building was standing. Eleanor's evidence was intact. We did it, Eleanor, she thought, the relief nearly painful. Justice is finally coming.

"Annie."

Jack was in front of her.

She hadn't heard him cross the lobby. He stood close now, his injured arm bound, his face pale beneath the grime and sweat, but his eyes were bright with something that stole her breath. "You saved us," he said quietly. "You saved everyone." She shook her head as her hand found his.

"We did. All of us. Eleanor. You. Me. She started this. We just finished it."

Agent Chen approached with Sarah Mitchell in restraints, her tailored control finally fractured. Sarah's hair had come loose. Her blouse was torn. But even now, calculation lingered behind her eyes.

As Agent Chen read her rights, Sarah's gaze fixed on Annie. "It's not over," she said softly. "You think you've won, but this goes deeper than you understand. Eleanor's little story will be a nuisance. Nothing more."

"It's not a story," Annie replied. "And it's not just hers anymore."

She pulled the birth certificate from the portfolio. "We know about the baby. Thomas Blackwood Jr. Born March 12, 1927. The rightful heir your great-grandfather murdered."

For the first time, real fear touched Sarah Mitchell's face. "That's impossible," she whispered. "There was no child."

"There was," Annie said steadily. "And we're going to find out what happened to him."

As federal agents led Sarah away, Annie felt something finally settle inside her—an ache easing that she hadn't realized she'd been carrying. Eleanor was no longer a ghost. She was a witness.

But even as the lobby filled with medics and bomb technicians and shaken survivors, Annie knew one truth remained unresolved. Richard was the murderer.

But an empire like this didn't rise by one man's hands alone. Who else had helped make Eleanor's child vanish with her?

***

Jack sat in the passenger seat of Agent Chen's unmarked SUV as they pulled away from First National Bank, the flashing lights of emergency vehicles painting the afternoon in fractured streaks of red and blue.

He turned in his seat as far as his injured shoulder would allow and watched through the rear window as bomb technicians in heavy protective gear disappeared back into the building Annie had saved from destruction.

The bank looked deceptively unchanged from the outside—brick walls still standing, windows reflecting sunlight, the flag over the entrance still stirring in the breeze. No one passing on the sidewalk would guess how close it had come to becoming a grave.

His shoulder throbbed with every movement, a deep, grinding pain that reminded him of just how close he had come to being another casualty in a long line of people who had crossed the Mitchell family. The earlier gunshot wound had been bad enough.

The fight with Sarah Mitchell had reopened it, twisted it, pushed it past what the doctors would have ever approved. He was almost certainly looking at surgery and months of physical therapy.

But he was alive.

Annie was alive.

And Eleanor Blackwood's voice—nearly erased, nearly silenced forever—had finally been heard.

Jack let his head rest briefly against the seatback, closing his eyes as the adrenaline drained from his system, leaving exhaustion in its wake. For the first time since the break-in at Annie's shop, since Uncle Eric had been found bleeding on the kitchen floor, since fire and bullets and pursuit had become their daily reality, there was nothing he needed to react to.

No immediate threat. No decision that had to be made in seconds.

Only the long, slow reckoning that followed survival.

"Any word from EOD?" he asked quietly, opening his eyes again.

Agent Chen glanced at him from the driver's seat before returning her attention to the road. "They've confirmed multiple charges throughout the lower and main levels. Military-grade components, remote triggers, redundant systems. Whoever built them knew exactly what they were doing. If Annie hadn't found that override..." She shook her head once. "We wouldn't be having this conversation."

Jack turned, looking back at Annie.

She sat in the rear seat, her knees drawn slightly inward, both hands resting over the leather portfolio that held Eleanor's evidence. The adrenaline had left her too, and the color had drained from her face, but there was a steadiness to her posture that hadn't been there before. Not shock. Not fragility. Resolve. The kind that came after walking straight into terror and refusing to let it win.

She caught him watching her and gave a small, tired smile.

It hit him then—harder than any bullet ever could—that he had almost lost her. Not in some abstract, distant way, but in the most immediate sense possible. He had stood in that lobby believing he was about to watch the building collapse with her still inside. He had accepted that. Had made peace with it in the only way he knew how: by deciding that if she was going to die, he would die first.

The realization left him cold.

"What happens now?" Annie asked, breaking the silence. "With the evidence. With Sarah Mitchell. With all of it."

Agent Chen exhaled slowly.

"Now we build the case. A real one. Not just against Sarah Mitchell, but against the entire structure that's protected her family for decades. Eleanor's ledgers alone give us a financial trail that spans nearly a century. Money laundering, shell companies, bribery, contract killings. We'll be opening federal investigations in at least three states by morning."

Jack watched the road slide past the windshield, small towns and side streets blurring together. "And her people?"

"Already being picked up. Raids are underway at multiple locations. Safe houses. Business fronts. Storage facilities. The hospital assault and the bank attack gave us probable cause to move fast."

Annie shifted slightly, her fingers tightening around the portfolio. "And Thomas."

The name hung between them.

Thomas Blackwood Jr. A child who should have grown up heir to a family legacy. A child whose existence had been erased so completely that even Eleanor's own descendants hadn't known he'd lived.

"Finding him—or his descendants—is going to be difficult," Agent Chen said carefully. "Birth records from that era are inconsistent. Adoption registries were private, often manipulated. And if Richard Mitchell arranged for the child to disappear..."

"...then he made sure there was no trail," Annie finished.

Jack nodded. "But Eleanor planned for that too. She preserved what she could. Names. Doctors. Financial anomalies. It's not nothing."

"No," Agent Chen agreed. "It's not."

Jack leaned back, the motion pulling a tight breath from his chest. "If Thomas survived... if he had a family... we're talking about people who've lived their entire lives without knowing who they were. Without knowing what was taken from them."

"And if he didn't survive," Annie said softly, "then at least the truth will finally be known. No more erased children. No more lies."

Jack studied her profile, the way exhaustion softened her features without diminishing their strength. She had walked into the fire for this truth. Crawled through tunnels. Stood in front of explosives with seconds on the clock. Not for money. Not for revenge. But for a woman she'd never met. For a child who had never been allowed to grow up.

"There's another layer to this," he said slowly. "If Eleanor's son has living descendants, and if they establish a legal claim, then the Mitchell family fortune becomes subject to forfeiture. Businesses. Properties. Investments. That's going to impact people who had nothing to do with Richard Mitchell."

"That doesn't make the inheritance legitimate," Agent Chen replied.

"No," Jack agreed. "But it does mean the fallout will be massive."

Annie didn't hesitate. "Justice usually is."

Jack looked at her then, really looked, and felt something settle inside him. She wasn't naïve about what they'd started. She wasn't blinded by righteousness. She understood the cost. And she was still willing to pay it.

His phone vibrated in his pocket.

He startled at the sound, then pulled it free, surprised to see his mother's name on the screen.

"Mom?"

"Jack." Her voice broke on his name. "We saw the news. The bank. The explosion. Are you hurt? Is Annie with you?"

"We're both okay," he said, meaning more than just physically. "Shaken. But okay."

A breath he could almost feel left her lungs. "Thank God."

"How are you and Dad?"

"We're fine. The agents are still here, but they say the woman behind it all has been arrested. They're very serious people, Jack. They don't look like anyone you'd want angry with you."

He managed a faint smile. "That's usually a good sign."

There was a pause. “Your father hasn’t stopped thanking God. And I haven’t stopped praying for you since you drove away.”

Jack closed his eyes briefly. “I’m sorry I scared you.”

“You’ve scared me your entire life,” she said gently. “It’s part of loving you.”

He swallowed. “Mom... I need to tell you something.”

“I know.”

He opened his eyes, glancing back at Annie. “Do you?”

“You love her,” Maggie said simply. “And she loves you. And you’ve both been afraid for a long time.”

Jack felt emotion press behind his eyes, sudden and unexpected. “It took almost dying for me to stop running.”

“Then I’m grateful you didn’t die,” his mother said. “And I’m grateful she didn’t let you.”

He exhaled a soft, almost broken laugh. “We’re coming out to the ranch when this is over. If that’s okay.”

“Dinner will be waiting,” Maggie said without hesitation. “And your old room is exactly as you left it. I refuse to believe any son of mine is permanently grown.”

“I love you.”

“I love you too.”

When the call ended, Jack kept the phone in his hand longer than necessary, staring at the dark screen as if it might offer something more.

Home.

For years, the word had carried weight. Loss. Regret. The ghost of a future he had once believed in and then deliberately destroyed. Now, for the first time since Lily's death, it felt uncomplicated again. Not a place haunted by what might have been. A place waiting.

He lifted his gaze to Annie once more and found her already watching him—not with worry or fear, but with quiet recognition, as if she saw exactly where his thoughts had gone and was standing there with him in them. "We're going to have a lot of interviews," Agent Chen said. "Court appearances. Evidence processing. And you, Detective, are going to have a very stern conversation with an orthopedic surgeon."

Jack huffed quietly. "I'm looking forward to it."

"And after that?" Annie asked.

Jack didn't answer right away.

After that meant the silence after sirens. The days without threat. The life that had been postponed for four years by grief and guilt and fear.

After that meant choice.

He turned in his seat as much as his shoulder allowed. "After that, we stop letting dead people dictate what the living are allowed to have."

Annie held his eyes.

"And what are we allowed to have?" she asked.

He didn't reach for her. Not with agents in the car. Not with adrenaline still fading and everything raw. But his voice didn't waver.

"A future," he said, "one that isn't built on fear."

She nodded once, the small motion heavy with meaning, and outside the window Fairview slid past in the late-afternoon light—ordinary, unaware, alive—while behind them a century-old lie was collapsing and ahead of them the truth was finally free, and for the first time in years Jack didn't feel like he was bracing for impact; he felt like he was moving forward.

Chapter 19

ANNIE KNOCKED SOFTLY ON Uncle Eric's hospital room door, her heart heavy with the weight of what she was about to reveal. The past few days had passed in a blur of federal interviews, sealed warrants, forensic teams, and media speculation as Sarah Mitchell's criminal organization was systematically dismantled piece by piece.

Agents moved in and out of Fairview. Bank records were seized. Assets were frozen. Names that had once carried quiet local respect were suddenly spoken on the evening news, alongside words like racketeering, domestic terrorism, and generational conspiracy.

But through all of it, Uncle Eric had remained here—removed from the chaos by necessity, recovering from his injuries, shielded from the full truth by doctors' orders and federal caution. He knew Sarah Mitchell had been arrested. He knew the attack on Annie's shop and the fire had been intentional. He even knew Eleanor Blackwood's murder had finally been proven.

What he didn't yet know was that everything he thought he understood about his family—and his own place in it—was about to change.

"Come in, sweetheart," his voice called, stronger now than it had been since the attack.

Annie stepped inside and closed the door gently behind her. Uncle Eric was sitting up in bed, color returning to his cheeks, his glasses perched on his nose as he worked his way through a folded newspaper.

The bandages around his head were smaller now, less ominous, and the monitors beside him beeped with steady reassurance instead of urgent warning. He smiled when he saw her, the same familiar, quiet smile that had anchored her since childhood.

Agent Chen followed Annie into the room, carrying a thick federal folder tucked beneath her arm.

"You look like you're about to give me either very good news or very bad news," Eric said, setting the paper aside. "And judging by the company you brought, I'm guessing it's not simple."

Annie crossed the room and took the familiar chair beside his bed. "It's not simple," she agreed. "But it's important. And you deserve to hear it from us, not from a lawyer or a news report."

Agent Chen inclined her head politely. "Mr. Whitaker, thank you for agreeing to meet with us. What we recovered from Eleanor Blackwood's safe deposit box, along with what we uncovered during the investigation, directly involves you."

Uncle Eric's brow furrowed. "I assumed it might. Given what Joy used to say about her mother, I always figured the truth would eventually circle back to the family." He glanced at Annie. "Did you find proof? Proof of what really happened to Eleanor?"

"We did," Annie said. "But we also found more than that."

She reached into her bag and carefully removed a protective document sleeve. Inside it was Eleanor's will, the paper preserved despite its age, her precise handwriting still sharp and deliberate across the page.

"Uncle Eric," Annie continued, steadying her voice, "Eleanor did have a son. Thomas Blackwood Jr. He was born three days before she was murdered."

Eric's breath caught audibly. "A son," he repeated. "Then he would have been the rightful heir. Richard Mitchell's entire claim—"

"—was a lie," Agent Chen finished. "And it was secured through murder."

Annie swallowed. "Richard Mitchell didn't just kill Eleanor. He killed her baby too. Thomas Jr. was five days old. The death certificate lists the cause as injuries sustained during violent assault."

For a long moment, Uncle Eric didn't speak. His gaze dropped to the blanket folded across his lap, his hands slowly curling into it as if anchoring himself to the present.

"A newborn," he said finally, his voice barely above a whisper. "He murdered a newborn child."

Annie reached for his hand. "Yes."

The word hung between them, heavy with everything it contained—grief, horror, the weight of a century built on blood.

"That man stole an entire life," Eric said. "Two lives. And then he stole everything that came after."

Annie slid Eleanor's will into his hands. "When Eleanor realized she and her son were in danger, she wrote this. She left everything to her daughters—Mary and Joy. She stated clearly, in her own words, that Richard Mitchell had no legitimate claim to the Blackwood estate."

Uncle Eric adjusted his glasses and began to read. Annie watched his face as he followed the lines, saw grief give way to stunned comprehension, saw the moment when meaning finally crystallized.

"This means..." he began.

Agent Chen spoke quietly. "Mr. Whitaker, based on Eleanor Blackwood's will, the financial records she preserved, and what our forensic accountants have traced through the Mitchell empire, you are the rightful heir to the Blackwood estate."

He looked up sharply. "Heir?"

"To the businesses, the properties, the trust holdings," Agent Chen continued. "Our current estimate places the value between sixty and seventy million dollars."

The words sounded unreal even to Annie, and she'd already heard them twice.

Eric stared at them. "Sixty million dollars," he repeated, faintly.

"The Blackwood operations expanded significantly after Richard Mitchell took control," Agent Chen explained. "Mining interests. Timber. Commercial real estate. Investments. Generational portfolios. It was built carefully, legally on the surface, but fueled underneath by laundering, extortion, and organized crime partnerships.

Now that the fraud has been exposed, those assets revert to their rightful ownership."

"To you," Annie said gently.

Uncle Eric leaned back against his pillows, shaking his head once, slowly. "I taught sophomore

Chen laid out the legal and financial implications of the Blackwood inheritance.

Sixty to seventy million dollars. Generational assets. Corporate holdings. The dismantling of a criminal empire. It was the kind of revelation that had unmade people Jack had interviewed before—men who grew euphoric or panicked or suddenly ravenous for control.

Uncle Eric did none of that.

Instead, he asked about the victims. About foundations. About how Eleanor's story would be told. About how to make sure what had been stolen was used to repair what had been broken.

This is where Annie gets her strength, Jack realized. This is where she learned that justice matters more than comfort. That truth matters more than profit.

He stepped closer to the bed, drawn into the gravity of the moment. "Mr. Whitaker," he said quietly, "there's something I think you need to be prepared for. This doesn't end with paperwork.

There's going to be media attention. Court proceedings. People who come forward claiming family connections or business interests. Some of them honest. Some of them very much not."

Eric regarded him with clear, untroubled eyes. "Detective, I spent nearly forty years managing classrooms full of teenagers. I've handled rumors, manipulation, entitlement, and emotional meltdowns over broken pencils. I think I can survive a few lawyers and reporters."

Agent Chen laughed softly, and Jack felt the tension in the room ease by a degree. There was something profoundly stabilizing about Uncle Eric—his quiet humor, his refusal to be overwhelmed, his instinctive centering of people over assets. It was exactly the temperament this inheritance needed.

"There's another layer," Jack continued, his voice turning more serious. "Sarah Mitchell's organization was larger than we initially believed. While we've arrested the primary figures, there are still financial beneficiaries out there. Business partners. Corrupt officials. People who profited from the Mitchell operations without ever getting their hands dirty."

Annie turned toward him, concern shadowing her eyes. "You think there's still danger?"

"I think there are people who won't be happy to see this money change hands," Jack said carefully. "And people who won't want Eleanor's evidence fully exposed in court. Uncle Eric inheriting this fortune threatens some very powerful interests."

Agent Chen nodded. "We're already seeing indications of that. Several of Sarah Mitchell's financial associates have disappeared since her arrest. We've intercepted communications suggesting there are individuals who would prefer the Blackwood claim... not exist."

Eric's mouth tightened. "What does that mean for Annie?"

"It means continued federal protection," Agent Chen replied. "And private security, once the estate transfer is formalized. This kind of inheritance attracts attention. Not all of it benign."

Jack watched Annie absorb that information, saw the conflict in her expression—the relief that Eleanor's truth had survived, and the sorrow that it would continue to carry danger with it. He knew that look well. It was the look of someone who accepted the cost of justice without ever resenting it.

"Uncle Eric," Jack said, then paused, aware that what he was about to say didn't belong to the investigation. It belonged to the future. "There's something else you should know. Annie and I... we're not just partners anymore."

Eric's gaze shifted between them, and then his mouth curved into the first true smile Jack had seen since the attack. "Son, I figured that out the moment I watched the two of you try to pretend you weren't terrified of losing each other."

Jack felt heat touch his face, but he didn't look away. "I'm planning to ask her to marry me, sir. Assuming she'll have me after everything I put her through."

Eric's smile deepened. "About time. Annie's been carrying a torch for you long enough that I was starting to worry it would scorch the furniture."

"Uncle Eric," Annie protested, her face coloring.

He waved it off gently, then turned back to Jack, his expression shifting into something quieter, more solemn. "Annie is the most important person in my life. She's smart, stubborn, compassionate, and brave to the point of recklessness. She's also been hurt. I won't stand by and watch anyone do that to her again."

Jack met his gaze without hesitation. "Neither will I. I love her. I've loved her for years. And I intend to spend the rest of my life proving that."

Eric studied him for a long moment, the silence weighted but not uncomfortable. Then he nodded. "Good. Because with this inheritance coming into the family, Annie's going to need someone she can trust without question. Someone who loved her before any of this existed."

Jack glanced at Annie, saw the emotion shining unguarded in her eyes, and felt something settle inside his chest that had been restless for far too long.

Agent Chen cleared her throat politely, drawing them back toward practicalities. "We should also discuss the administrative side of this transition. Mr. Whitaker, you'll need financial advisors, legal counsel, and representation for the media. There will be interviews. Statements. Court proceedings."

"I want Annie involved in all of it," Eric said immediately. "She's the one who found the locket. She's the one who preserved the evidence. Any decisions that come from this, she has a voice."

Jack felt a surge of pride as he watched Annie's reaction—not surprise, but quiet acceptance of responsibility. She had never shied away from the truth. She wouldn't start now.

"There's one more thing," Jack said, pulling his phone from his pocket. "The story's already starting to break. Uncle Eric, you're about to become very famous."

Eric sighed, then shook his head. "Well. I suppose there are worse ways to be known than for helping uncover the truth about a murdered woman."

As the conversation shifted to logistics—attorneys, temporary housing, protective details—Jack found his thoughts drifting back to Eleanor Blackwood. To a woman who had hidden truth in metal and ink because she believed the future could be better than her present.

To a woman who had trusted that one day, someone in her family would be stubborn enough, brave enough, and decent enough to finish what she had started.

Looking at Annie and Uncle Eric, Jack knew she had been right.

Now it was their turn to carry what she had preserved—and to make sure the justice she had waited nearly a century for truly mattered.

Chapter 20

THREE WEEKS LATER

Annie stood at the floor-to-ceiling windows of the law firm's conference room, watching late-morning traffic crawl through downtown Nashville.

The city looked exactly as it always had—people heading to work, delivery trucks easing into loading zones, pedestrians weaving through crosswalks with coffee cups in hand—ordinary life continuing as if nothing monumental had happened. And yet, nothing in her own world felt ordinary anymore.

Three weeks had passed since Sarah Mitchell's arrest. Three weeks since Eleanor Blackwood's evidence had been carried out of a bank vault and into the hands of federal prosecutors. Three weeks since Uncle Eric had learned that the quiet life he'd built as a high school history teacher rested atop a legacy stolen through murder nearly a century earlier.

Annie still hadn't fully wrapped her mind around it. Some mornings she woke, expecting the weight of the locket at her throat to be nothing more than a strange dream.

Some nights she lay awake replaying the sound of the countdown timer, the way the numbers had glowed red against the marble walls, the way Jack's voice had cut through the chaos like an anchor.

Behind her, the low murmur of voices filled the conference room. Attorneys, financial advisors, forensic accountants, and federal investigators worked through what felt like an endless sea of documents—ledgers and asset reports, incorporation filings and court orders.

All of it showing the slow, careful movement of money that had begun with Richard Mitchell's crime and grown into a criminal empire disguised as respectability. The long mahogany table was crowded with neatly stacked folders and open laptops, each page another piece of Eleanor's story being returned to the light.

"Ms. Whitaker?"

Annie turned from the window at the sound of David Morrison's voice. The estate attorney stood near the end of the table, holding out a thin folder. "We're ready for your signature on the foundation documents."

She crossed the room to where Uncle Eric sat, glasses perched on his nose, his once-familiar legal pad replaced by documents that would have overwhelmed most people. He looked tired, but steady—still healing physically, still adjusting emotionally, but present in a way that told her he was meeting this new reality head-on.

"You sure about this?" Annie asked quietly as she reviewed the papers. "This represents giving away almost fifty million dollars."

Eric's mouth curved into the same gentle smile she remembered from childhood, the one he'd worn when she'd panicked over missed homework assignments or broken friendships. "Annie, sweetheart, what exactly would I do with fifty million dollars? Buy a fleet of fishing boats and spend the rest of my life learning how to sink them?" He shook his head.

"Eleanor didn't preserve that evidence, so her family could live in luxury. She preserved it so the truth could stand. So justice could matter."

Annie swallowed past the tightness in her throat and signed her name beside his, the pen feeling heavier than it should have. The Eric Whitaker Foundation for Victims' Rights. Legal aid. Trauma counseling. Financial assistance for families navigating the aftermath of violent crime. It wasn't wealth he was claiming. It was responsibility.

"The remaining assets will be placed in a family trust," Morrison explained. "Enough to ensure long-term security, but structured to preserve the principal for future generations."

"And the legitimate Mitchell businesses?" Annie asked. "The ones not directly tied to criminal activity?"

"They'll continue operating under new management," Morrison replied. "We've identified several ethical firms interested in stabilizing the companies and protecting the employees while severing all prior associations."

Before Annie could respond, the conference room door opened and Agent Chen entered, a thick folder tucked beneath her arm. The expression on her face carried the particular satisfaction of someone who had spent years dismantling shadows and was finally watching them collapse.

"I have an update," she said, taking a seat beside them.

Annie felt her pulse quicken. "Good update or complicated update?"

"Both," Agent Chen replied. "Seventeen additional arrests in the past ten days. Financial crimes, weapons trafficking, contract violence, political corruption. Eleanor's records gave us a road map, and Sarah Mitchell's cooperation confirmed it. The network was broader than we initially suspected."

"And Sarah?" Uncle Eric asked.

"She pled guilty to federal racketeering charges in exchange for testimony. Life without parole. Her cooperation has already opened investigations in six states."

Annie exhaled slowly. It still stunned her how one woman's courage—ink on paper, metal locked inside a locket—had been enough to unravel nearly a century of violence.

"What about ongoing threats?" Annie asked. "Are we still... targets?"

"The immediate threat has been neutralized," Agent Chen said. "But given the scope of what's been exposed, we're recommending continued security for the next year at minimum."

Annie nodded. Safety, she'd learned, wasn't the absence of danger. It was the presence of vigilance.

"There's something else," Agent Chen added, reaching into her folder. "Something I think you'll want to see."

She laid a photograph on the table.

It was the Blackwood family portrait—but not as Annie had first seen it, yellowed and faint, faces blurred by time. This version was larger, clearer. The forensic imaging team had restored it, enhanced its resolution, coaxed detail back from the edges of loss.

Annie leaned closer.

Eleanor's face emerged with startling clarity. Not just her features, but her expression. She wasn't smiling for the sake of a camera. She was looking directly at whoever stood behind it with an intensity Annie felt in her own chest.

"She knew," Annie whispered. "Even then."

Agent Chen nodded. "There was also something else. An inscription on the back we couldn't read before."

She turned the photo over.

In careful, slanted handwriting:

For my daughters and their daughters, and all who come after them. May you always remember that truth is stronger than fear, and love is stronger than death.

March 1927.

Annie pressed her fingers to her lips as tears blurred the words. Eleanor hadn't just hidden the evidence. She had left a blessing.

"She really did know," Uncle Eric said softly. "She knew she might not survive—but she made sure her love would."

Annie's hand moved instinctively to the locket resting against her heart. "What do you think she'd say if she could see this?" she asked. "The arrests. The foundation. Everything her truth has set in motion."

Eric studied the photograph a moment longer. "I think she'd say the waiting was worth it."

Agent Chen nodded. "And I think she'd be proud of what you're doing with what she preserved."

As Annie looked around the conference room—at the documents, the professionals, the quiet machinery of justice finally turning in the direction it should have taken a century ago—a sense of completion settled into her bones. Eleanor's voice had been heard. Her killers exposed. Her legacy reclaimed.

And it wouldn't end here.

It would continue in courtrooms and classrooms, in counseling offices and legal aid clinics, in families who would never know Eleanor's name but would benefit from her courage.

Thank you, Eleanor, Annie thought, touching the locket once more. Thank you for trusting the future.

Outside the windows, Nashville moved on in sunlight and sound, unaware that a century-old lie had finally fallen.

But Annie knew.

And somewhere beyond the reach of time and violence, she believed Eleanor Blackwood did too.

***

Jack adjusted his tie for the third time as he stood outside the law firm's conference room, watching blurred shapes move behind the frosted glass. His shoulder still ached when he overdid it, a dull reminder of how close he'd come to not standing here at all, but today wasn't about injuries or investigations.

Today was about the future—about the life he wanted to build with Annie now that the past had finally loosened its grip on both of them.

The small velvet box in his jacket pocket felt impossibly heavy.

He'd been carrying the ring for a week, turning the moment over in his mind again and again, waiting for a pause in the chaos that never quite seemed to come. Every day brought new developments—court hearings, asset transfers, foundation meetings, security briefings.

Annie's world had expanded overnight into something vast and complicated, and Jack had found himself wondering when it was fair to ask her to take on one more life-altering decision.

Maybe there's never a perfect time, he thought. Maybe you don't wait for the ground to stop moving. Maybe you just choose who you want to stand with while it does.

The conference room door finally opened, and Annie stepped out, her expression tired but lighter than he'd seen it in days. Uncle Eric followed behind her, already surrounded by attorneys and advisors offering handshakes and quiet congratulations. The foundation documents, it seemed, were officially complete.

Jack moved to Annie's side as they headed toward the elevators. "How did it go?"

She released a slow breath that sounded almost like a laugh. "Uncle Eric is officially one of the most generous philanthropists in Tennessee. Fifty million dollars to help victims of violent crime." She shook her head slightly, still amazed. "I think Eleanor would approve."

"I think she would too." He studied her face, the faint shadows under her eyes, the steadiness beneath the exhaustion. "And how are you holding up? With all of this—the money, the attention, the way your life keeps reinventing itself?"

They slowed as they reached the elevator bank. Annie was quiet for a moment, considering the question honestly. "Some days I feel like I'm living someone else's life. Three weeks ago I was arguing with suppliers and worrying about whether my shop could make rent. Now I'm helping manage a foundation and meeting with federal prosecutors."

Her mouth curved, but her eyes stayed thoughtful. "I don't know if I've caught up yet."

The elevator doors opened, and Jack waited until they were alone inside before speaking again. "And how do you feel about things settling down? About the protection easing eventually. About whatever normal looks like now."

Annie leaned back against the mirrored wall. "I'm not sure I remember what normal is," she admitted. Then she straightened slightly, her expression shifting. "But there is something I wanted to tell you. About the foundation. About what Uncle Eric and I decided."

Jack felt a flicker of nerves he hadn't expected. "Okay."

"We want you involved," she said. "Officially involved." She met his eyes.

"Jack, you understood Eleanor's case in a way almost no one else did. You risked your life to protect the evidence, and the people connected to it. We want you on the foundation's board. Helping us identify cases. Families who need resources. Who needs someone to take their search for justice seriously?"

For a moment, he couldn't speak. The offer landed somewhere deep, touching the part of him that had never really known what to do with the things he'd seen, the losses he'd cataloged, the dead who rarely got voices. This was a way to keep doing the work—without losing himself in it.

"Annie," he said slowly, "that means more than you know." Then he drew a breath, feeling the weight in his pocket, the timing he'd been circling. "But there's something I need to ask you before we talk about anything else. Something I should have asked you four years ago."

The elevator chimed softly as it reached the ground floor. Neither of them moved.

Jack reached into his jacket and took out the small velvet box. Annie's breath caught, her hand lifting instinctively to her mouth as recognition dawned.

"Jack..."

"I know this isn't perfect timing," he said, the words coming faster now. "Your life is complicated. Mine isn't exactly simple. But Annie, I spent four years letting fear make my decisions. Fear of loss. Fear of loving you. Fear of what it might cost." He swallowed. "I'm done with that. I don't want another day that isn't honest."

He lowered himself to one knee on the elevator floor and opened the box. The diamond was simple, unpretentious, catching the fluorescent light in a way that felt almost symbolic—quiet brilliance, no spectacle required.

"Annie Whitaker," he said, his voice steady even as his heart raced, "you are the bravest person I know. You see truth where others look away. You fight for people who don't have anyone else. You make me want to be better than I am." He held her gaze. "Will you marry me?"

For a heartbeat, she didn't move. Then she was pulling him up, arms around his neck, tears warm against his skin as she laughed and cried at the same time.

"Yes," she said, her voice fierce and breathless. "Yes. Of course, yes."

Jack slid the ring onto her finger, his hands not quite steady, and drew her into a kiss that tasted like relief and certainty and something finally set right. When they broke apart, he rested his forehead against hers.

"I love you," he said quietly. "I've loved you for years. I just finally learned how to stop running from it."

"I love you too." Annie lifted her hand between them, studying the ring as if it might disappear. Then she looked back at him, a familiar spark in her eyes. "You're really sure about this? About marrying into a family that apparently attracts century-old murder mysteries?"

Jack laughed softly, thinking of caves and vaults and locket chains slick with blood, of Eleanor's careful handwriting and the way Annie had run toward danger instead of away from it.

"Annie, if Eleanor taught us anything, it's that some things are worth the risk. That love doesn't protect you from loss—but it gives the loss meaning." His fingers brushed the locket at her throat. "And I can't think of anything I want more than a life with you in it."

They finally stepped out of the elevator and into the Nashville sunlight, the city bright and ordinary around them, unaware of what had just been promised in a mirrored box between floors.

As they walked, Jack felt a deep, unshakeable gratitude settle over him—to Eleanor, whose courage had outlived her; to Uncle Eric, who had raised Annie with a quiet devotion to what mattered; and to the strange mercy of second chances.

The future waited, uncertain and full, and Jack knew there would be other cases, other shadows, other costs.

But whatever came, he wouldn't be facing it alone.

And that, he knew, made all the difference.

Chapter 21

Six Months Later,

Annie stood at the front of the small mountain chapel, her hand resting in Jack's, feeling the steady warmth of him beside her as sunlight filtered through stained-glass windows and scattered soft color across the wooden floor. The air smelled faintly of pine and wildflowers, carried in from the open doors behind the last row of pews.

Outside, the Tennessee mountains rose in gentle layers, timeless and unmoved, as if they had been waiting for this moment just as patiently as she had.

Six months ago, her world had been built of questions and danger, of blood on tile and secrets buried in silver. Now it was built of quiet certainty, of a man standing beside her who had seen her at her most afraid and never once stepped away.

She listened as Pastor Williams spoke about love, commitment, and the courage it took to build a life with another person. The words floated through the chapel, meaningful but secondary to the deeper awareness anchoring her in place. This wasn't the beginning of something fragile. It was the continuation of something tested.

When Jack turned fully toward her, emotion clear in his eyes, Annie felt the weight of the past year settle into something solid and sure. They had fought together. They had bled, feared, uncovered, and nearly lost everything.

They had also found each other again in the middle of it, not as they had been four years earlier, but as they were now—changed, scarred, and unafraid to choose each other anyway.

When the ceremony reached its conclusion and the final words were spoken, a hush fell over the chapel before breaking into warm applause. Annie felt Jack's hand tighten around hers as they turned to face the people who had carried them through the darkest weeks of their lives.

Uncle Eric sat in the front pew, his shoulders squared, his eyes bright with unshed tears. He looked older than he had a year ago, but steadier too, as if the truth they had uncovered had given him something deeper than inheritance ever could. Jack's parents sat beside him, their expressions open and joyful, relief softening the edges of everything they'd lived with since Jack's line-of-duty shooting years earlier.

A few rows back, Agent Chen watched with a rare, unguarded smile, no longer an investigator coordinating a crisis but a witness to what had grown out of one.

Scattered among family and close friends were others whose lives had intersected with Eleanor's story—officers who had worked the case, investigators who had helped dismantle the Mitchell organization, even a few of the bank employees who had survived the final confrontation. People who understood, in different ways, what it had cost to reach this day.

As Annie and Jack walked back down the aisle together, the sound of celebration filling the chapel, Annie's gaze was drawn to the small table near the front. Resting beside the unity candle was a framed photograph Uncle Eric had placed there earlier that morning.

The restored image showed Eleanor Blackwood seated with her daughters, her expression composed, her hand resting protectively on a child's shoulder. Beneath the glass, faint but legible, was the message Eleanor had written in March of 1927.

Truth is stronger than fear. Love is stronger than death.

Annie slowed, just for a breath, meeting Jack's eyes before looking again at the photograph. They had done what Eleanor had waited for someone to do. They had carried her story into the light. They had made it impossible to erase again.

The reception was held at the Calloway ranch, the same place where fear had once ruled the nights and headlights on gravel had meant danger. Now white lights hung from the porch railings and across the open lawn, glowing softly as music drifted through warm evening air. Laughter rose and fell like a tide, mingling with the low sound of crickets and the distant call of night birds.

Food crowded long tables. Children ran through the grass. Conversations overlapped in easy, ordinary ways that felt almost miraculous after months of whispered plans and guarded movements.

When Uncle Eric stood to speak, the crowd gradually quieted. Annie felt emotion tighten her chest as he talked about the years after her parents' deaths, about watching her grow into a woman who refused to look away from hard things, about meeting Jack and recognizing the kind of man who would stand beside her instead of in front of her.

As he lifted his glass, Annie realized how much of what they had survived had led them not only to justice, but to community. Eleanor's story had not ended in a courtroom. It had expanded outward, touching lives and drawing people together who might otherwise never have known each other.

Later, Annie found herself standing at the edge of the celebration, watching Jack dance with his mother while Uncle Eric entertained a cluster of children with exaggerated stories. The foundation had already begun its work. Three families were receiving legal assistance. Two cold cases had been reopened.

The past was no longer only something to mourn. It was something that could be answered.

Agent Chen joined her, glass in hand, her posture relaxed in a way Annie hadn't seen before the arrests. They spoke briefly about the trials ahead, about testimony and evidence and the slow machinery of justice, but there was a sense of finality underneath it all. The danger was over. The truth was secured.

When Jack returned, slipping his arms around Annie from behind, the world felt reduced to the simplest of facts: the warmth of him, the quiet strength in his embrace, the shared understanding that they had crossed something and would never go back.

"What are you thinking about, Mrs. Calloway?" he asked softly.

The name still felt new, like something fragile she was learning to hold, but it fit in a way nothing else ever had.

"I'm thinking about how far this story traveled," she said. "How long it waited. And how many people it took to finish."

Jack rested his chin against her hair. "And we did."

"We all did," she corrected gently. "Together."

Later, when the music softened and the crowd thinned, Annie touched the locket at her throat, the silver worn smooth by time and by her fingers. It had been her something old, resting over her heart as she promised her life to Jack. Once it had held secrets and fear. Now it held memory.

Not of violence. Of courage.

The night deepened around the ranch, the mountains dark and steady beneath the stars. There would be more cases. More work. More days shaped by the foundation and by the truth they had chosen to carry forward.

But tonight was not about that.

Tonight was about standing in the aftermath of something finished and realizing that what remained was not loss, but space. Space to build. Space to love. Space to live.

And as Annie rested her head against Jack's shoulder, listening to the quiet of a place that had once been filled with threat and was now filled only with music and light, she knew that Eleanor's long vigil had ended not in silence, but in the beginning of something that would endure.

***

Jack stood on the ranch house porch, loosening his tie as he watched the last of the wedding guests disappear down the long gravel drive, their taillights blinking briefly before being swallowed by the dark.

The music had faded; the laughter had drifted back into the house, and the wide pastures that had glowed with lantern light only an hour earlier were settling into quiet again. The reception had been everything he'd hoped for—warm, unguarded, filled with the kind of joy that didn't demand attention but lingered, gentle and real.

He drew in a slow breath of night air scented with grass and honeysuckle and something deeper, earthier, that always reminded him he was home.

"Best day of my life," he said when Annie stepped onto the porch beside him.

She had changed out of her wedding dress into jeans and one of his shirts, the sleeves rolled, her hair loose down her back. The sight of her like this—comfortable, familiar, his—hit him with a quiet force that was somehow stronger than the moment she'd walked down the aisle.

"Mine too," she said, settling into the porch swing and tugging him down beside her. "Though six months ago, I never imagined I'd be married to a detective and helping run a foundation for victims' rights."

"Six months ago, I was convinced I was too damaged to ever do this," Jack replied honestly, slipping an arm around her shoulders and drawing her close. "Funny how life refuses to stick to the stories we tell ourselves."

They let the swing rock gently, the rhythmic creak of chains blending with the distant chirr of insects and the soft sigh of wind moving through the trees. Below them, Fairview lay scattered across the valley, a constellation of quiet lights that looked almost unreal from this distance.

Earlier, those same pastures had been crowded with people who had nearly lost Annie, nearly lost the truth, nearly lost each other. Now there was only stillness.

Jack felt it settle into his bones, not empty but full.

His parents had insisted they spend the night at the ranch before leaving for their honeymoon, as though this place needed to close the circle before something new could begin.

In the morning, they would fly to Scotland, a trip Uncle Eric had offered without hesitation and Annie had accepted with wonder, talking excitedly about ancestry records and old villages. Jack smiled at the thought. Of course, she'd turn a honeymoon into a research project.

"Jack," Annie said quietly, shifting just enough to look up at him, "do you think we'll keep doing this? Solving cases, helping families, working through the foundation?"

He didn't answer right away. Instead, he watched the slow blink of a distant porch light, thought about cold evidence rooms and restless nights, about the way Annie saw connections other people missed, about the way she never looked away from what mattered even when it terrified her.

"I think mysteries have a way of finding people who care," he said finally. "And I think we've already proven we don't know how to walk away when the truth is at stake."

She nodded, thoughtful. "Eleanor's case wasn't the end."

"No," he agreed. "It was proof."

The word seemed to resonate between them. Proof that they could survive danger without losing tenderness. Proof that the past didn't have to own the future. Proof that love could grow in the middle of darkness and not just in its absence.

Jack rose and offered her his hand. "Come on, Mrs. Calloway. Let's go inside and start our married life."

She took it, smiling, but instead of letting him pull her toward the door, she tugged him back until they were both standing at the edge of the porch, facing the open sky. Annie took his hand, but instead of letting him lead her inside, she tugged him gently back toward the edge of the porch.

The mountains rose in dark, quiet layers beneath a sky scattered with stars.

"Jack," she said softly, "do you think it's really over?"

He knew what she meant. Not the wedding. Not the foundation. The case.

He followed her gaze across the land, thinking of vaults and ledgers, of blood on kitchen tile, of a woman who had hidden the truth because she believed someone, someday, would finish what she started.

"I think the investigation will go on," he said carefully. "There will be trials. Appeals. Paperwork that never seems to end. But Eleanor's case? The truth of what was done to her, who did it, and why?" He shook his head. "That part is finished."

Annie let out a slow breath she'd been holding for far too long. "So we can finally stop chasing it."

"Yes." His arm tightened around her. "We did what we went looking to do. We found the truth.

We protected it. We made sure it couldn't be buried again."

She leaned her head against his chest. "Then she can finally rest."

The words settled between them, heavy but not painful. Not anymore.

"Eleanor spent her last days trying to make sure her story wouldn't disappear," Jack said quietly. "Now it won't. Her name is in court records. Her evidence is in federal custody. Her family's future is secure. There's nothing left for her to fight."

Annie nodded, her fingers curling into his shirt. "No more running. No more hiding. No more waiting."

"Exactly," he said. "The case is closed."

They stood there for a moment, not speaking, letting the stillness do what it needed to do. When Annie finally looked up at him, her eyes were clear in a way he hadn't seen since before all of this began.

"I love you, Jack Calloway."

"I love you too, Annie Calloway," he answered, the name still new and right on his tongue. "For the rest of our lives."

Only then did he lead her back toward the house, toward the light and warmth and the ordinary, extraordinary future waiting on the other side of the door.

Epilogue

March 3, 1927

The house was finally quiet.

Not the brittle silence of emptiness, but the softer kind—one Eleanor had learned to treasure. The kind made of sleeping children and banked fires and lamps turned low. Of the faint ticking of the mantel clock and the distant whisper of wind through the trees beyond the windows.

Night had settled fully over the hills, cloaking the Blackwood estate in shadow. Clouds drifted across the moon, leaving the grounds in alternating washes of pale light and darkness.

Eleanor stood at the foot of the narrow staircase leading to the second floor, one hand resting against the banister, the other curved protectively over her belly. The baby shifted beneath her palm, a slow, rolling movement that brought both comfort and ache.

"Hush now," she whispered, though there was no one to hear her. "Mama's here."

She had just finished putting the girls to bed.

Mary had fallen asleep first, thumb tucked beneath her cheek, curls fanned across the pillow. Joy had fought longer, her small hand clinging to Eleanor's nightdress, her questions tumbling one after another until exhaustion finally claimed her.

"Will you stay till morning?"

Eleanor had smoothed her hair and pressed a kiss to her temple. "I'll always be near."

Now they slept, unaware of the storm of thoughts that would not let their mother rest.

Eleanor turned away from the staircase and moved slowly down the hallway, careful with each step. Her body felt heavier at night. Not merely with child, but with something deeper. A pressure behind the ribs. A weariness that sleep did not touch.

Tonight more than most.

Richard's school friends were staying in the east wing—three boys, nearly grown, loud with false bravado and restless energy. Thomas had insisted they be made welcome. "Good for Richard," he had said. "Keeps him occupied."

Occupied.

The word tightened something in her chest.

They had taken supper earlier, filling the long dining room with careless laughter and clattering silverware. Eleanor had sat at the far end of the table, smiling when expected, listening without hearing, counting the minutes until she could retreat upstairs.

She had watched Richard from beneath her lashes, and he had barely looked at her—and that frightened her more than his attention ever had.

Now she walked unlit corridors, guided by memory and faint spilling of moonlight through tall windows. The floorboards were cool beneath her slippers. The walls seemed to hold their breath as she passed.

She did not go toward the cellar or the study, because there was nothing more to be done tonight. The letters were hidden, the accounts recorded, and the pieces quietly set where they would one day be found. The trap was laid. Whatever tomorrow held would come, whether she slept or not.

At the turn in the hall, Eleanor paused beside the window overlooking the back gardens. The moon had slipped free of the clouds, casting silver over the hedges and stone paths. For a moment, the world looked almost gentle.

She rested her forehead lightly against the glass.

"Lord," she murmured, the way she had so many nights before. "You see what I cannot. You know what waits where I cannot go. I place them in Your hands."

Her daughters, sleeping upstairs with their soft breaths and tangled curls, were the first faces in her mind. This child as well, still hidden beneath her heart, shifting as though aware of the danger that pressed so close.

Even Thomas—blind as he was to the threat within his own family, blind as he was to her fear—remained someone she longed to protect.

And herself, too, though she scarcely allowed herself to name that desire. She was a life God had made, a soul entrusted with breath and purpose, even if she had spent years learning to believe otherwise.

A strange calm moved through her then. Not peace exactly. But resolve. The quiet of a heart that has finished wrestling and chosen its direction.

She straightened and continued down the corridor.

As she neared the back stairwell that led to the family bedrooms, she heard muted voices drifting from the east wing—low, indistinct. Male laughter. A door closing. Footsteps moving away.

Eleanor slowed instinctively.

She told herself she was tired. That the house made its own sounds at night. That nothing was amiss.

Still, she waited until the voices faded before turning the corner.

The corridor beyond was dark, the lamps turned low. Shadows gathered thickly here, pooling in doorways and alcoves. Eleanor moved quietly, unwilling to draw attention, unwilling to disturb Thomas or the guests or anyone.

She wanted only her bed. Only the familiar weight of blankets and the quiet reassurance of walls that had always meant safety. She longed to lie in the dark and listen to the old house breathe around her—the soft ticks and sighs of settling wood, the distant whisper of wind through the trees.

The night had pressed heavily upon her, and weariness had sunk into her bones. She reached the first step of the narrow staircase that led to her room and lifted her foot, already imagining the small mercy of rest.

That was when she felt it.

Not a sound. Not a touch. Something else. A subtle shifting of the air, a change so slight it might have been imagined, and yet her body recognized it before her mind could reason it away. Presence.

Her breath caught painfully in her throat. She did not turn.

She told herself it was nothing—that fear had made her foolish, that the long day and the long weeks had frayed her senses. She told herself she was safe. She told herself—

A hand clamped over her mouth, brutal and unyielding. Another arm locked around her middle, crushing her back against a solid body and driving the breath from her lungs in a sharp, silent gasp. The world tilted violently. The stone floor seemed to spin beneath her feet as her slipper slipped.

She caught the scent of wool, of sweat, of something sharp and unfamiliar. Her heart slammed once against her ribs, then again, as her hand flew instinctively to her belly. The arm around her tightened. And the darkness closed in.

About the author

Rebecca Hemlock has been a Nancy Drew fanatic since childhood and is drawn to anything involving mysteries and story telling. Her books have realistic, complex characters who endure crime related hardships that either test their faith or spark a new found faith in God.

Each character follows the underlaying mission found in Romans 12:21. "Be not overcome of evil, but overcome evil with good."

An award-winning Christian Fiction author of more than 20 books, Rebecca began her novel writing career, after four years of working as a freelance journalist. She is an active member of The American Christian Fiction Writers and Sisters in Crime and loves writing for those who like historical elements mixed with their Romantic Suspense and Mysteries.

Rebecca has earned a Bachelor's degree in English and Creative Writing along with an Appalachian Studies certificate and plans to continue her writing education.

Want to read more from this author?

Get a free ebook when you sign up for Rebecca's Newsletter.
Scan the code and Sign Up today!

Made in the USA
Coppell, TX
18 June 2026

81399417R00184